blues for hannah

# blues for hannah

*a novel*

## TIM FARRINGTON

crown publishers, inc.
new york

Excerpt reprinted from Dante's *Divine Comedy*, volume II: *Purgatory*, translated by Dorothy Sayers (New York: Penguin Books, copyright © 1955). Used by permission of David Higham Associates.

Excerpts reprinted from *Love's Fire* (Ithaca, N.Y.: Meerama Publications, copyright © 1988) and *Speaking Flame* (Ithaca, N.Y.: Meerama Publications, copyright © 1989), re-creations of Rumi by Andrew Harvey. Used by permission of Meerama Publications.

Excerpt reprinted from "Snow White and the Seven Dwarfs," from *Transformations* by Anne Sexton. Copyright © 1971 by Anne Sexton. Reprinted by permission of Houghton Mifflin Company. All rights reserved.

Excerpts reprinted from *Light Upon Light: Inspirations from Rumi,* by Andrew Harvey, copyright © 1996 by Andrew Harvey. Used by permission of North Atlantic Books, P.O. Box 12327, Berkeley, Calif. 94712.

Excerpts reprinted from "Legend," "Ave Maria," "The Bridge of Estador," from *Complete Poems of Hart Crane,* Marc Simon, editor. Copyright © 1933, 1958, 1966 by Liveright Publishing Corporation. Copyright © 1986 by Marc Simon. Used by permission of Liveright Publishing Corporation.

Excerpt reprinted from "Little Gidding" in *Four Quartets,* copyright © 1943 by T. S. Eliot and renewed 1971 by Esme Valerie Eliot. Reprinted by permission of Harcourt Brace & Company.

Excerpt reprinted from *The Collected Works of St. John of the Cross,* translated by Kieran Kavanaugh and Otilio Rodriguez, copyright © 1979, 1991 by Washington Province of Discalced Carmelites. Used by kind permission of ICS Publications, 2131 Lincoln Road N.E., Washington, D.C. 20002.

Published by Crown Publishers, Inc., 201 East 50th Street, New York, New York 10022.
Member of the Crown Publishing Group.

Random House, Inc. New York, Toronto, London, Sydney, Auckland

www.randomhouse.com

CROWN and colophon are trademarks of Crown Publishers, Inc.

Printed in the United States of America

Design by Karen Minster

Library of Congress Cataloging-in-Publication Data
Farrington, Tim.
Blues for Hannah: a novel / by Tim Farrington.—1st ed.
I. Title.
PS3556.A775B58   1998
813'.54—dc21                                    97-40640
ISBN 0-609-60281-0

10   9   8   7   6   5   4   3   2   1

First Edition

for Lynn Mason

## acknowledgments

I am deeply grateful to Sue Carswell, my editor at Crown Publishers, for the vigor and freshness of her work with this book, and for her jubilant spirit. Thanks also to Greer Kessel for an early and generous reading, and to Rachel Kahan for her deft contributions. My ongoing gratitude goes out to Linda Chester, of the Linda Chester Literary Agency, for years of kindness, both personal and professional; and to Laurie Fox, *agent extraordinaire* and comrade-in-arms, for literary gifts beyond measure, and for the treasure of her friendship. I also owe particular debts of gratitude to Carl Wittwer for profound playfulness and the rapid cycle amplification of DNA; to LaDawn Haws; to Fir Emmanuel; and to my mother and father. And to my wife, Claire, who fills my life with joy, as ever, all my love.

Holy souls, there's no way on or round
But through the bite of fire: in, then, and come!
Nor be you deaf to what is sung beyond.

The Angel at the Pass of Fire
Dante's *Purgatory,* Canto xxvii

## one

# hannah's song

———

*The phone call came* this morning, just after four A.M. I let the machine get it, figuring it was a wrong number from the East Coast, but picked up when a troubled-sounding man with a flat Midwestern accent identified himself as Lucifer Burns of the something-something-something. It was all a little garbled through my answering machine's speaker and my grogginess, like a static-filled radio call from someone under enemy fire at the front. I half-expected the guy to say "Over" when he finished his sentence. I had been dreaming of something tangerine-colored, which seemed to have exploded.

"Yes?" I said dazedly. "Hello? Mr., uh, Burns?"

"Barnes," he said patiently. "Officer Lamar Barnes, of the Nebraska Highway Patrol. Are you Jeremiah Mason?"

This was a bad sign, as if there were not already enough bad signs in a four A.M. phone call from the police. Everybody calls me "Mason," except my family and my wife, who call me

"Jerry." Nobody calls me Jeremiah. How could you call a person Jeremiah on a daily basis? The name's too big for anything but suffering and vision.

"Yes," I said carefully, searching my mind for outstanding warrants in the Plains states, wondering how they'd found me in San Francisco.

"I'm afraid I have some bad news."

In a strange way, I was not surprised. Hannah always used to tell me that she was going to die in a fiery car wreck on a road in the Midwest. It was that specific, with her. She had known it, she insisted, from the age of twelve, when she was just picking up a guitar for the first time—as if it were a part of her early music education: the A minor pentatonic blues scale, bar chords, and an early death. I told her it was just her ambition talking, she wanted to be Buddy Holly and skip the work of a whole career, but she would say, "No, no, Buddy Holly died in a plane crash, this is a car wreck." So I'd say, "James Dean, then, you've got a James Dean complex." But she would say, "No, he died in California, and there was no fire. With me, there's fire."

*With me, there's fire.* She could see it so clearly it was irrefutable: on the road with her band, dozing in the passenger seat, on some endless night drive from a Bob Seger song to the next gig. And then she's awake, and the car is drifting out of control, headlights splaying somewhere off to the left, on a collision course with something solid, on some nowhere road in the Midwest. Boom, bam, blue and yellow flame.

She was always so goddamned cheerful about it, very fatalistic, very cool. "Wet wood burns slow," I would tell her, implying she'd survive any fire in her immature condition.

"Oh, it won't happen until ten or fifteen years after I really learn how to play the guitar," Hannah would say, unfazed, implying she'd be ready to burn by then. At eighteen, she still felt like she had all the time in the world.

And now she's pulled it off, and the cops are calling *me* at four in the morning. Of course: Hannah always had my name and current address on two pieces of laminated paper, one in her wallet and one in her guitar case. *In the event of an emergency please contact Jeremiah Mason at...* She labored to keep my phone number up to date through every twist and turn, and so for years, whenever the phone did ring, some archaic and utterly credulous part of my consciousness was expecting the worst. It lent real poignancy to life, I must say. I didn't believe her entirely, but I believed her enough. My real hope was to die before Hannah and have the cops call *her*. But that was just wishful thinking, whereas her vision—it seems—was true.

The wreck, of course, was self-fulfilling: passenger seat my ass. I had no doubt that Hannah was driving and forget those theories about dozing at the wheel. Hannah's flair for the visionary moment, the sweet God-given arc of dissolving light, got the best of her at last, that's all there is to it: She staged her own dissolving arc, hitting every mark on cue. She'd been biding her time for almost thirty years by the time she recognized that stretch of Nebraska road, practicing the tragedy in three-part harmony, accompanying herself on guitar, and it really pissed me off.

—

The first time I saw Hannah Johnson, she was sitting by the fireplace in my best friend Burton's grandfather's house, in a little college town tucked away in a valley in northern Utah. Burton's grandfather was out of town, at his summer shack in the nearby Wasatch mountains, praying to survive the Second Coming of Christ as one of the Elect. Burton, a mime and a biochemist, was twenty-one at that point and didn't give a hoot about the Apocalypse. He had decided to make the best of his grandfather's borderline-insane concern with ultimate things and throw a party in the old fanatic's absence.

The gang was all there—our college crowd, although I had dropped out of school the year before after picking a fight with my first-year watercolors teacher. I was still present in Utah mostly because of my own inertia, the beauty of the mountains, and my love for LeeAnne Young. LeeAnne, a sweet blond Mormon girl majoring in elementary education at Wasatch State, was also concerned with her place among the Elect, but she was willing to put her immortal soul on the line to sleep with me. She wanted to bear my young and would eventually go so far as to marry me, a move she has had ample cause and leisure to regret. But I'm getting ahead of myself here.

Hannah, with the autumn fire backlighting her coffee-dark hair into tendrils of auburn, had a guitar on her knee and was tuning up, to no one's great concern. She was new to our crowd, just arrived from Long Island, ostensibly to take advantage of Wasatch State's Natural Resources program. (The one-time agricultural college had been one of the first places in the country to offer a major in ecological studies, though at that point in the early seventies the program retained much of its original emphasis on the ecology of cows.) I forget how Hannah had come to be at the party at all. From the other side of the sofa and coffee table, my casual first glance had taken in only that she was young, indigo-eyed, and shy, cute enough but clearly a freshman, an eighteen-year-old in jeans and a baggy flannel shirt. Her sole attachment seemed to be to her musical instrument, God bless her. I lived for art myself at that point.

Anyway, I was stalled on the far side of the living room, beneath the looming, badly painted oil portrait of Burton's grandfather's own grandfather (another religious maniac, and husband to eight wives), arguing Cubism with Burton, that scion of maniacs. Across the room, I could see that LeeAnne had been similarly cornered by a grad student who was wearing one of those awful tweed jackets with the leather elbows. She and I smiled at each other ruefully, surrendered to our fates. Burton's perverse position was that Picasso and Braque had not taken Cubist technique far enough, that they had been on the verge of science and had backed off again into flimsy, slipshod beauty. A little more calibration of the fractured planes and they'd have had replicable neo-Riemannian results, a true geometry of perception. Seurat—he of the myriad tedious tiny points—was Burton's exemplar in this regard. Chromatic calculation and so forth, in a technical vein.

"So you believe the real mission of a painter is to fill in the dots on a color TV set—" I was saying to Burton, perhaps a little heatedly, as Hannah began to play her first song.

———

What can I say about that music? I'd be an idiot to try too hard to say anything; frankly, I'd just screw it up. And certainly there are precedents for a mystical reticence—if not incoherence—in such matters. The prophet Jeremiah, for instance (after whom I was named by my well-meaning parents, who were trying to put down some Old Testament roots in the somewhat neglected lawn of their suburban Catholicism): Called to his mission personally by God, Jeremiah stood before the Lord and stammered like a stricken child. Most translations have his first words in the Presence as something along the lines of *Ah, ah, ah!,* which actually sounds sort of awed, refined, and appreciative; but I believe the prophet probably said something more like "Duh." And that's about what I can muster when I try to stutter out why the music that night changed my life so thoroughly.

In any case, Hannah later repudiated the song as her art progressed, along with entire notebooks full of similarly beautiful songs from that era, as Picasso repudiated his Blue Period and Monet abandoned Argenteuil. In later years, you couldn't get her to play "White Empty Canvas" again on a bet. But I happen to love the early Picasso and Monet. (I burned all my own apprentice work, of course, scrupulously.)

*White empty canvas, so barren and hostile—*
*Lacking in feeling, you lay my soul bare. . . .*

I do recall, almost painfully, how the firelight moved on Hannah's hands as she played, a rich, harlequin dappling of rose and golden ocher. Hannah's voice, earthy and only faintly Long Island-inflected in song, seemed ocher to me too, though more toward the rust-orange end of the range: a sandstone warmth that glowed and capered and grieved like the fire, as the shadows on the bricks behind her gathered layers of lavender darkness into violet.

Or maybe I was hallucinating—certainly I would later try to paint that purpling effect and fail completely. All I can really say with certainty is that the fire's dance and the music were somehow related, harmonizing with all the colors present while Hannah's voice moved toward a perfect peace in a minor key, and that it seemed to me an entirely worthy project to squander the rest of my mortal days considering the subtleties and richness of that single instant. I was, as they say, a goner.

Let me add here and now that there were drugs present at the party—it was the mid-seventies and an unemphatic strain of marijuana had reached even northern Utah—but I had done no drugs. There was hard alcohol present, booze aplenty, but I was drinking the mildest beer, in deference to LeeAnne's strong views on the demon rum. I was sober, in a word. My life turned on a sober dime.

—

*The light is burning me,*
*God, how it's blinding me,*
*Just like that white empty canvas*
*whose captive I am.*

When the music stopped, it took me a moment to realize that Burton was still talking. He was still on Seurat, something about complementary hues: Apparently you could do the whole thing on a fucking slide rule. A *lot* of people were still talking, actually; the party went on more or less normally all around me, like a nightclub where the feeble act onstage has been the merest backdrop to the usual business of seduction and intrigue. Apparently the zone of sacred and eternal stillness into which I had entered had been a private experience.

From the wall above me, Burton's ancestor looked down sternly on it all. Blessed with eight wives, he radiated no contentment whatsoever. The painter, I noted, had cheated on the strict black backdrop, introducing some enlivening emerald and dark purple. And who could blame him, really? Burton's great-great-grandfather on his own had an aura that could choke the moon.

"Yeah, yeah," I said impatiently to Burton. "What a load of crap." And I crossed the room to where Hannah sat.

"Who wrote that song?" I asked her, hoping against hope that it was Judy Collins, or Jackson Browne, or some obscure

Dylan in a lyrical, folkie vein: someone I could admire from a decent distance without tearing the fabric of my life.

Hannah looked startled, then met my eyes with her cool, blue gaze and smiled.

"I did," she said.

In bed that night with LeeAnne in her apartment near campus—my own bohemian painter's life was based at that time out of a more or less uninhabitable barn loft studio north of town—we talked cautiously about the party. LeeAnne was in a bit of a state herself, having spent much of her night at the party embroiled in debate with a zealous grad student working on his thesis in Skinnerian psychology, which was all the rage then. The grad student's strong jaw and confidence had shaken LeeAnne's naive and really quite charming faith in freedom and dignity. Rats and pigeons and variable rate reinforcement—the reduction of the soul's activity to pecking for treats had all seemed pretty straightforward, suddenly; and by the end of the party the Elect had begun to tremble in their heaven and salivate on cue.

"I'm wondering what education actually *is*," LeeAnne confided uneasily. "I'm wondering about my relationship to God. Is it just a reflex?"

I fondled her warm breasts contemplatively. "Think of this theory as a virus that will pass soon."

"The statistical results seem indisputable."

"Uh-huh," I said, and continued with my reflections, running my tongue south between her breasts across the salty-sweet landscape of her belly. LeeAnne's perfect skin held its summer tan excitingly all the way through October and I was feeling a little neo-Pavlovian myself, despite a Postimpressionist hangover from my rounds with Burton and the nagging awareness that I was still humming "White Empty Canvas." It was clear enough to me that I had been overly impressed by a freshman with a guitar and would be trying to catch the indigo of Hannah Johnson's eyes at the easel first thing the next morning. But these are the sort of things that occasionally complicate any healthy sex life.

My tongue found LeeAnne's belly-button and lingered briefly, causing her to giggle, as it always did.

"A conditioned response," I noted.

LeeAnne stiffened. "Jerry, this is serious stuff."

"It certainly is." I moved on, downstream, as it were, toward the delta. But LeeAnne had turned chilly, her body's luscious tributaries freezing into impassability. My lack of respect for academic ephemeralities always pissed her off. I gave up hope for a superficial physical solution and returned my head to the nonsexual altitudes.

Beyond the bedroom window a half-moon showed hazily over the mountains, through a thin high cloud cover that promised snow before the colored leaves were even off the trees. The fleeting glory of Rocky Mountain autumns always grieved me deeply.

In bedrooms on either side of us, Mormon college girls slept soundly in flannel nightgowns of pink and damask rose.

LeeAnne's apartment mates disapproved of me almost entirely, on principle and in practice, though I did my best to charm them. Their deep religiosity found little to admire in the suspect arts. I wondered again what I was doing in Utah.

We were silent for a long moment. LeeAnne kept her windows open to the vigorous night air according to a bracing notion of health. I could see my breath in the moonlight, condensing before us and settling on the quilt. Somewhere in the depths of the house the inadequate furnace heaved ineffectually. And still I was humming "White Empty Canvas."

"I thought that new girl's song was nice, didn't you?" I remarked, too casually.

LeeAnne's ears pricked up. She saw it all first, I have to say: Her female radar noted the blip long before my simpler male equipment had registered a thing. I was still convinced at that point that what I felt for Hannah Johnson was, at most, appreciation.

"Very nice," she said, the note clipped perfectly to let me know she thought I was full of shit.

It was all ahead of us then. Was there a way out of the pain to come? Would I have taken that way even if I'd seen it? I know the simple truth: I'd have chosen the flames, love's unimaginable road through fire, without hesitation. My soul had recognized a partner and the details were a matter of time. But my choice would—inevitably—have been naive. You can never feel the pain ahead of time.

And now, two decades later, Hannah's dead at thirty-nine, gone too soon in a blaze of glory, as she always thought she would. The story's mine to tell. And so I'll say it now, while I'm still dizzy with the freshness of the loss: It was worth it, every idiot step I took into deeper pain. And I'd do it all again, the whole foolish dance, starting here, starting now, just to hear Hannah's fingers on those strings, and see her eyes in the autumn firelight.

# burning music #17

Heart, be brave; if you cannot bear grief, go—
Love's glory is not a small thing.
Come in if you are fearless;
Shudder, and this is not your house.

Rumi

---

*LeeAnne was in bed* beside me, rousing slowly from her usual fathomless sleep of the just, as I handled the call from the cop. Not *still* in bed with me, strictly speaking, after more than twenty years of high melodrama and sexual combat, separations and reunions, the brutal ins and outs of the heart; but undeniably in bed with me again. If you calculate anniversaries according to the strict accumulation of time together, LeeAnne and I are somewhere back among the silk/linen gifts and pearls, in the low- to mid-teens. The legitimate celebration of our silver anniversary will have to wait for a new kind of math to be developed. We do, however, qualify for the purple heart of damaged togetherness, with oak-leaf clusters.

In any case, there she was: LeeAnne the patient and the kind, LeeAnne the phoenix, Saint LeeAnne of hopeless causes, patroness of the unlikely survival of love, getting the picture in pieces and exclamatory scraps from my end of the conversation and sitting up a little more in bed at each fresh revelation. By the end of the call she'd turned her lamp on and was fully upright, propped on two fat pillows, looking sick at heart.

According to Officer Barnes, Hannah's westbound van had somehow crossed the dividing line on a perfectly featureless stretch of two-lane road and found a tractor-trailer coming east. The truck driver had come out of it with a chipped tooth and a headache, but everyone in the van, Hannah and the rest of the Blue Flame Band—her boyfriend and co-lead guitarist Pete Michaels, their bass player Juanita Delacruz, and their drummer Jim "Beat" Bedderman—had died more or less instantly, just after three A.M., Central Time.

"And what time is it there now?" I asked—a little irrelevantly, perhaps, but I was still trying to get oriented. I'd only been in bed since a little after two A.M. myself, after failing well into the wee hours to get a certain purple right on the mess that was my canvas-in-progress.

"A little after six," the officer answered kindly. "We held off for a while—I wanted to wait until a decent hour to call you. I know how disorienting it can be to wake up to news like this."

"Actually, it's four in the morning here."

"Damn," the guy said. "Right, right, *west coast*. I can never get that time-change thing right."

There was more, but the upshot was clear enough. Somebody was going to have to identify Hannah's body and take it home to Long Island, and Hannah had been telling me for almost a quarter of a century by now to keep her family out of it. She had been on distant terms with her father for years; I was the only number in her wallet. I told Barnes I'd be in Nebraska by early afternoon and hung up the phone.

"So Hannah finally got her car wreck," LeeAnne said, her tone precise and uninflected: noting it, merely, for the record.

This was my thought exactly, of course, though it still made me mad to hear her say it. Somewhere deep inside of all of us is a half-baked hope that death will give us some respite from the truth, if nothing else. But death just makes the truth stand out like a skull on desert sand.

"Yeah," I conceded wearily. "She got her wreck." I turned away, climbing from the bed to reach for my paint-spattered jeans, then paused, caught by a random fashion scruple, wondering what would actually be appropriate dress for a Nebraska morgue.

From the bed, LeeAnne watched me attentively, sensitive to my mood. The curve of her belly showed like a rising half-moon past the crumpled ridge of the rich burgundy blanket. Seven-and-a-half months pregnant, she was the picture of a contented mother-to-be, except for the fact that she is sure to this day that I would rather have had her abort. It has been a great pain between us since her announcement this past spring. And there is some truth in her sense of it, I confess.

Certainly my heart sank at the news. I had considered a vasectomy after my son Samuel was born in the late eighties, and my first thought when I heard that LeeAnne was pregnant was a wish that I had gone through with the operation. I never said a word, but I'm a bad actor and LeeAnne is no fool. It has not made for a joyous pregnancy.

"I'm afraid I have to go to Nebraska," I said, striving for a calm and businesslike tone.

"Of course you do," LeeAnne agreed, impeccably, very supportively—on cue, as it were. Of course I had to go. It was the reasonable thing to do.

And I began to sob, because somehow, if LeeAnne agreed I had to go, then Hannah was really dead.

—

I must have painted Hannah's face twenty times in the days after the party at Burton's grandfather's house, trying to get the color of her eyes just right and to be faithful to the fire and the deeper violets in the shadows beyond the hearth. I suppose I was trying to get God into it too, that stillness at the heart of the moment that had turned me upside down. And, I admit, to keep the hard evidence of lust to a minimum.

I was aiming way too high and inevitably the thing evolved toward abstraction, then collapsed under its own weight. By the end of a humiliating week or so I had managed to piss that dangerous blue away into something playful, fresh, and clever, if not profound: a depth in the canvas like the shallow end of a swimming pool, surrounded by cartoon whirls of graffiti flame and a subtle lavender darkness, the whole thing framed in brick-red and all too reminiscent of Miró. A self-mockery, as I saw it, a private joke on me; and a fever-sweat, the outcome of a brief obsession. I called it *Burning Music #17,* laid it against my studio wall with the rest of my visionary botches, and got back to what I was really trying to do on canvas then, which was make the Rocky Mountains disappear into a neo-Sung gray wash.

It was left to Burton, then, to get to know Hannah first. She showed up at one of his mime troupe's practices not long after the party at his grandfather's house. Burton had formed the troupe in his freshman year to address the cultural vacuum at Wasatch State, and he and his white-faced crew were constantly feeling their way around inside invisible cages in the Ag Building lobby, or chasing each other through the Student Union in super-slow motion, dressed in body stockings, while business-as-usual went on at normal speed all around them. Hannah, fresh-faced and aglow, was intent on refining her body language, which her guitar teacher had told her could use some work. Burton, the Henry Higgins of body language—or perhaps the Machiavelli—obliged, and everything he told her seemed like a revelation. Hannah had never given her body language a second thought. It was like learning French for her, in white-face.

In the long run, to be honest, everything she learned was more or less wasted: Hannah's body language would never be anything but very frank, with a slight Long Island accent. She just wanted to play the damned guitar, leaving the nuances to her music, and to hell with the way she sat on the stool. As total opposites, however, she and Burton fell almost instantly into one of those incandescent affairs that flares on the horizon briefly like the northern lights or a nuclear test and then is gone, leaving everyone in the flatlands baffled. Burton kept the relationship secret for the week and a half that the good part lasted. By the first time I saw the two of them together, the honeymoon was over. And so I met Hannah for the second time.

—

The three of us gathered for lunch in Hannah's dormitory cafeteria, ostensibly because Burton wanted her to begin to meet his friends, but actually because the relationship was already in desperate need of props. Burton, as usual, had played the whole affair so close to his vest that I was stunned and I confess a little dismayed to realize that his mystery woman was the young guitar player from his grandfather's hearth. I thought I had already dodged that bullet. But here she was again, in the flesh. As I began formulating the coincidence story in my mind—Burton's new girlfriend, you'll never guess, and so on—I could already hear LeeAnne's deft inflection: *Oh, how nice.*

Still, the introductions went well enough. I was struck anew by Hannah's indigo eyes. I'd failed completely, I saw at once, to catch the shade on canvas. The firm, yet delicate, line of her jaw had also escaped me. Her face had an off-beat near-beauty that with a little attention and determination might have laid men low in every direction, but Hannah was never much for plucking her eyebrows and the rest of the glamorous disciplines. If you didn't love her soul without makeup you were not going to get in the door. She took my hand in a warm strong grip and met my gaze as calmly and confidently as a tiger might, despite body language that said a host of irrelevant things about how Burton had described me to her beforehand as a viciously antisocial painter of dubious morals.

"I was humming that song of yours for about a week after the party," I told her, in the liberty of the first moment.

"Oh?" Hannah said, lighting up. It pleased her almost excessively. But the context clearly forbade any excess. This was Burton's lover, after all, and his own unmistakable body language—perhaps ever so slightly smug—had already conveyed to me his delight with her. I was bound by friendship to conduct myself with due reserve. And for that imposed restraint, I was genuinely glad. LeeAnne and I were not in the best of phases just then. She had signed up for a Psych 110 class after her run-in with the Skinnerian and all our recent conversations had been flavored uncomfortably with a rampant reductionism. But I was not looking for trouble. (I say that now, having managed nevertheless to find trouble at every turn in my path.)

For her part, Hannah seemed innocent of any troublesome intent. She was more slender than I had remembered, and a little uncertainly balanced without her guitar, as befitted an underclassman and new girlfriend. She wore a baggy wool sweater the color of Montauk sand, with a line of chocolate brown hearts dancing breast-high across the front—a gift, I assumed, from her parents—and aside from the tiger-calm of her eyes seemed mild enough in every way. She still had a trace of white greasepaint just below her ear—the two of them were fresh from shocking the bourgeoisie in the Student Union plaza. Burton's mime troupe did their radical best every day from noon to 12:25, though the social order seemed generally unperturbed.

We moved through the cafeteria line with our plastic orange trays, gathering our food. Burton, intent on "subtilizing his energy," was on some kind of all-fruit diet at that point. He was trying his best to become invisible to normality, in the service of his art, and heaped his tray with apples and bananas. But Hannah went for the full American array, including mashed potatoes. I settled for a roast beef sandwich and a bowl of bright red Jell-O.

The three of us made our way out to a table by the big plate-glass window. Burton and Hannah sat side by side with me facing them and I could see right away that the two of them were in trouble. Hannah kept calling him "Burt," for one thing. You could no more call Burton "Burt" on a sustained basis than you could call Jean-Paul Sartre "Jack." Burton had devoted himself to deepening the natural chasm between himself and such familiarity. But Hannah persisted, almost touchingly, in trying to bridge the gap. She called him "Burt," and "Burtie," and even "B.R.," as if he were a cowboy poet or something. I could see her growing more baffled and frustrated with him throughout the conversation.

"You can't really mean that, Burtie," she kept saying.

"What makes you think I intend to *mean?*" Burton replied, perhaps a trifle gleefully.

I decided it was better to concentrate on my sandwich. Burton baffled almost everyone he met. He had the sort of face onto which you projected profundity, a lean, smart face, as open as a child's. But he had staked out the postmodern surface and he believed in his heart it was all just atoms knocking about. The rest was irony and style. He was a nihilist wrapped in an enigma, which usually drove people a little nuts, and so I was not surprised to see it driving Hannah nuts.

In any case, it was romantic fallacy this and cultural relativity that, with Hannah's sense of beauty's relevance increasingly offended. She argued for truth pure and simple, for Keats and Muddy Waters, her voice growing louder as Burton's grew cooler. The table trembled; I watched my Jell-O quiver in its little bowl as they grew passionate. We were starting to draw some uneasy looks from the neighboring tables. Outside the window, a light snow had begun to fall and the mountains already had that fairy-dusted look of early winter at its dreamiest.

"Now, now—" I said, assuming a grandfatherly tone to try to cool them down.

Hannah ignored me. Burton himself, taking the entire argument as improv theater, seemed perfectly prepared to let it run its course. His deftly nuanced body language conveyed a high Stoic serenity colored slightly with amusement, which only frustrated Hannah more.

"It's all some kind of fucking game to you, isn't it?" she demanded of Burton.

He reached for a banana and began to peel it. "Does that make you angry?"

Hannah's fingers tightened briefly on her knife handle. She had exquisite hands, tanned and strong and graceful—a craftsman's hands.

"Angry? No. A little disappointed, maybe. Silly me—I actually thought for a while there that you had some balls."

Burton met my eyes impassively across the table, one brow raised slightly, as if to say, *Isn't this interesting?* Burton loved the human drama deeply, albeit from the distance of a Martian anthropologist.

"God, there's no point talking to you," Hannah exclaimed in disgust. She stood up, tossed her knife on her plate, and simply walked out the door.

The people at the tables around us relaxed. Burton sipped at his iced tea; I looked at my own plate as if it were a still life painted in another time and place and marveled at civilization's tenuous hold.

We were silent for a moment. Burton picked up the knife, reached for Hannah's plate, and cut himself a bite of her Salisbury steak. He chewed briefly, then cocked his head at me, amused, and said, "I really don't see the broad appeal of this."

"For Christ's sake, Burton," I said disgustedly, and got up to go comfort Hannah.

"She'll cool down soon enough. Those sweet young notions of hers can't possibly hold up."

"That's what I'm afraid of," I told him, as I left. I'd had the same damned fight with Burton a hundred times myself.

Outside the cafeteria, snow continued to fall. I shrugged my inadequate Goodwill windbreaker up to my ears and followed the freshest set of footprints straight across the lawn, between the tall twin dormitory buildings—men's on the right and women's on the left—and then through the parking lot toward the town cemetery. Every room on the north side of the dorms had an unobstructed view of the graveyard, an apt little *memento mori* in my opinion, though I doubt it changed many business majors to philosophy. And the philosophy classes at Wasatch State were thin gruel anyway. It was one of the reasons I'd dropped out so quickly. No amount of language analysis and the later Wittgenstein was going to get you through that brutal moment at three A.M. when you realize that nothing you have ever done meant shit.

Sure enough, one clean set of new prints showed on the whitening lawn beyond the cars. Hannah had made for the traditional hole in the cemetery's south fence, used by generations of morbid underclassmen and lovers looking for some empty grass. I ducked in after her where the ground was still bare beneath the evergreen canopy of junipers, pines, and Engelmann spruce that made the graveyard's western reaches such a haven. Her tracks stopped where the trees began.

I stopped beside the monument to a Utah pioneer named Pierce and listened. At first there was nothing to be heard but my own breath. It was snowing hard now. The soundless flakes settled steadily on the gravestones beyond the trees. Half a mile to the east, the mountains were invisible, lost in swaddling gray-white, an effect I'd been trying for in dilute inks all fall. The air was dense with silence.

I was already beginning to wish I'd brought my sketchbook. There were some fantastic lines emerging as the snow made all the cemetery's edges and granite planes stand out. And then I spotted Hannah. She was sitting not too far away with her back against an old Rocky Mountain juniper, bent over a pocket notebook, a pen in her hand. Her flight into the cemetery, it struck me, had not been as precipitate as my pursuit: Hannah, at least, wore a sturdy blue parka.

I walked over to her. She glanced up at me briefly, not quite scornfully, but not encouragingly either. Then she turned her attention back to the notebook page. I settled back on my heels and waited. It seemed too intrusive to ask her if she had any more paper, though I would have robbed for some just then. But I was also feeling strangely content.

The quiet in the trees was like the quiet of an empty church. Some snow was slipping through the branches now and a few flakes were melting slowly in Hannah's dark hair. To my right, a series of granite gravestones of descending size all read "Billsley." The smallest one, closest to me, said, *John Robert Billsley. b. March 7, 1924. d. March 8, 1924.* The end of the Billsley line, it seemed.

At last Hannah finished the first draft of whatever she was writing and looked up at me.

"I suppose you're going to tell me Burton's feelings are hurt or something, and I should rush back and apologize?"

"Actually, he was eating the rest of your lunch when I left."

"Asshole."

This was indisputable. I held my tongue. Hannah turned her attention back to her paper.

"What are you working on there?"

"A song," Hannah replied, with a child's absorbed simplicity, as if I were an idiot to have to ask.

She went on with it for quite a while, ignoring me pointedly, humming a little from time to time to work out the chord progressions. I sat across from her with my back against a hundred-fifty-year-old juniper, beside the graves of the Billsley clan—still wishing, from habit, for some paper and charcoal, but really quite content just to be there with Hannah while that beautiful snow fell all around us. It must have been cold but I don't remember the cold. I was extremely young myself at that point and it seemed to me too that art sufficed. I was just glad she let me stay. Perhaps I even began to love her there, seeing how bent she was on turning hurt to music.

—

"Was she okay?" Burton asked me when I saw him the next day. He was a little guilty and anxious for once about his own philosophical excess. I think that Hannah was the first girlfriend he'd ever had that he would notice losing.

"More than okay," I told him and left it at that. "A Hole in Your Soul" was already written, after all, a blast in C major, three verses and a chorus on the heartless intellect. Certainly there was no sense rubbing Burton's nose in how capable Hannah seemed of living without him, or how much I wanted to sleep with her myself by then. The world brings all our bad news to us soon enough anyway.

## three

## the footprints of the ox

Beauty is a simple passion,
But, oh my friends, in the end
You will dance the fire in iron shoes.

Anne Sexton, "Snow White and the Seven Dwarfs"

**Continental had a flight** into Omaha by way of Houston leaving at seven that morning: Through the severe triangulations of the airport hub concept I could be in Nebraska by two o'clock that afternoon. I began to toss clothes indiscriminately into a bag and look for my shaving kit. LeeAnne shuffled off to the kitchen to start a pot of coffee, looking like something out of an "I Love Lucy" rerun in her massive terrycloth bathrobe and the faded house slippers with the funny pointed toes that made it seem as if her legs ended in two giant red opossums.

Not that I looked any better—I had put off my decision on the blue jeans and was still wearing my baggy sleeping boxers with the hearts on them. These had been given to me by LeeAnne on some happier Valentine's Day years before and, like so many fresh romantic gestures, had passed into the frayed half-consciousness of domestic use.

When I had finished the small chore of packing socks and civies, I was compelled to face the trousers issue again. If clothes really make the man, I do not amount to much—two decades of the most resolute artistic failure have left me as ill-equipped for funerals and weddings as I am for job interviews. The choice came down to my ubiquitous paint-spattered jeans and a pair of natty khaki slacks (also given to me by the ever-hopeful LeeAnne) that make me look like an aging Yale divinity student: nothing suitably dark, nothing sober, nothing with even the look of stability.

While I pondered the embarrassment of reaching forty without a scrap of decent clothing to my name, the door across the hallway eased open, and my son Samuel peered out, blinking at a world suspiciously astir at four A.M. Seeing me in my ridiculous boxer shorts and socks, he took heart and crossed the hall to our bedroom door.

"Is it the end of daylight savings time?" he asked. Sammy at the age of eight has grappled long and hard with the concept of daylight savings time. He wears his Space Navigator watch all the time, has known how to dial the number for the time on the telephone since he was three, and felt betrayed last spring when they switched the clocks on him. I can only sympathize, my own relationship with temporality being suspect and shaky.

"No," I said. "I have to go on a trip."

"What for?"

I suppose it is the moment every parent dreads, when you are overwhelmed yourself and they need a simple answer. *Because I have a weakness for music, son, and always did. Because God demands it, apparently. Because, Samuel, however delightfully love warms you when you start out, it will take everything before its flame is through.* How do you begin to explain to your child that you took one step down a road with someone, and then another, and then another, and then so many that maybe it's not a road at all anymore and maybe it never was and certainly not the road you started on and that at this point you are just baffled and broken and grieved and afraid it all meant nothing, but you still have to fly to Nebraska to identify the remains?

It was clear to me that I couldn't tell Sam anything while I was standing there in my shorts. I hung the khakis back in the closet and reached for my blue jeans. Decision made—if things like this can really be called decisions. It was too late to be anything but the paint-spattered idiot I was. I was going to tell him the truth, of course. Though I would rather have broken my back.

Sammy eyed me as I pulled the jeans on—alert but not wary, used to his old man's extremes. He looks just like Hannah. There's no way around it—the same searching indigo eyes, the delicate determined jaw. He has her nose, her ears, her smile—he has her *hands* already, which awes me. People exclaim that he's got my ash-blond hair, but that's no blessing: He'll just look like Hannah when he's balding at thirty-five. My own mild hazel eyes, my glowering Irish brow, my Roman nose, are nowhere to be seen in my son, though he has my thin physique and contemplative air, which already draws the bullies. And of course those who don't know the story often try to find LeeAnne in Sam, which is invariably upsetting.

With my pants on at last, I took a deep breath. "Listen, Sammy, there's something I've got to tell you."

Sammy nodded, frowning and scrunching up his eyebrows slightly to indicate seriousness.

"It's something very sad and very hard to understand."

"Did someone die?"

So much for my delicate approach.

"Someone did die, yes. Hannah died."

Sammy took it in somberly but without visible reaction, which is his way. He'll notice something, learn something, see something, and it's as if it dropped into the deep part of a lake. He's like an oyster with a piece of grit. It scares me to death, but LeeAnne says he's just like me. (Sammy calls LeeAnne "Mommy," by the way, and he's always called Hannah "Hannah," though he understands the concept of biological motherhood perfectly well. He just has always had his own sense of where to put the weight.)

"It was a car wreck," I continued. "Her van crashed into a truck."

Sam nodded. His nose was peeling—we'd been to the beach the day before and he'd washed all his sunblock off in the first ten minutes. We'd played dolphin derby in the frigid water until we both turned blue, and had hot dogs afterward.

"She'd been playing music with her band and they were on their way to play some more music. She was doing exactly what she wanted to do, and what God wanted her to be doing, and she was never afraid, Sammy. It's important that you never forget that."

He nodded again. We sat for a moment in silence, on the edge of the bed. I was leaning forward, elbows on my knees, hands clasped in front of me, and I noticed that Sammy was leaning forward in exactly the same way, though his feet were not quite touching the floor: skinny elbows on his knees, his small, perfectly-formed Hannah-hands clasped in front of him. Because he didn't know what to do, of course, and he thought that I did, and that it involved sitting like that. But I didn't know what to do either.

At last Sam blurted, *"Where?"*

I looked at him. "Where did she die, you mean?" He nodded. "In Nebraska."

"Nebraska," Sammy repeated. I watched him take it in, in and in and down and gone, like a stone into a lake. But it was clear enough to me that it would be a long time before he came to terms with Nebraska.

—

In the kitchen, the coffeemaker was gurgling over a half-filled pot. LeeAnne had the big frying pan out to scramble tofu eggs. It seemed inconceivable to me that I would ever eat again, but LeeAnne has survived her entire adult life with her belief in the importance of breakfast intact. Death is no excuse for poor nutritional habits. She was chopping some green onions as Sammy and I came in, shuffling back and forth between the stove and the cutting board, a vision in terrycloth, her red slippers screaming for replacement. I had given her those slippers myself, more or less as a joke, ten years before, early in the attempt at cohabitation that had preceded this attempt at cohabitation. Or maybe there was an attempt in between as well; I lose track sometimes. We had been living then in an apartment in the Richmond district that was all hallways, more or less, just several vast lengths of cold hardwood floor that grew clammy in the interminable fogs of the San Francisco summer. We couldn't afford rugs but the slippers were $3.98 at Walgreens, one size fits all. The things had a quirky honeymoon charm for about fifteen minutes, as I recall. I really had only bought them to get a laugh out of LeeAnne on a gloomy Wednesday and to celebrate our love surviving poverty and inclement conditions. But LeeAnne loved the slippers and wore them all the time. To my dismay, they symbolized some mythical coziness to her, a domestic tranquility our lives together too often failed to achieve.

Seeing LeeAnne shuffle faithfully around the kitchen in the slippers now, it occurred to me that I might have grown fond of the silly things. No doubt sudden grief had made me overly susceptible to poignancy.

"Well, well, look who's up," LeeAnne exclaimed cheerfully, seeing Sammy, who blinked in the brighter kitchen lights and smiled back uncertainly. "Mr. Early Bird himself."

"I already told him," I said, before she confused the kid with too much normality.

"Ah," LeeAnne responded in a tone that suggested, *Do you really think that was wise?* But she moved at once to take Sammy in her arms, a swift, instinctive swoop of comforting enclosure, as if he had just come in bloodied from a baseball game or bike wreck. Sammy promptly burst into grateful tears. He had just been waiting for the chance, it seemed. I stood apart, marveling as I often do at LeeAnne's touch with him, glad that poor Sam had one parent at least who knew how to let him be a kid whose mother had just died. While he sobbed on her shoulder, I moved to the stove to stir the eggs before they began to burn. I still wasn't the least bit hungry, but it seemed like a shame to let all that good energy of LeeAnne's go up in smoke.

The meal imposed its measure of the ordinary. LeeAnne and I discussed the practical side of my sudden departure. Someone was coming by my studio that afternoon, ostensibly to pick out a painting, my first potential sale in a month and a half; he would have to be rescheduled. Also, I had three works hanging in a restaurant in Oakland that were going to have to come down by Friday, as the owner's girlfriend had recently started a career in watercolors and he wanted the space. Also there was dry cleaning I had promised to pick up that LeeAnne would have to see to herself—she was giving a seminar that weekend on reincarnation and needed her red presenter's outfit. One of the ironies of LeeAnne getting sidetracked into checking out the Skinnerians was that one thing had led to another for her, psychologically speaking. She'd gone through Freud and the cognitive therapists and the medical theorists with their prescription pads at hand; had a small nervous breakdown before mastering in Erik Erikson; found Jung in California and taken some mescaline and a Ph.D. in Buddhist psychology at the California Institute of Integral Studies. Ultimately she arrived at a view of the soul so expanded that she could see even the behavior of pigeons in a Skinner box as part of a coherent cosmic mind. Now people pay three hundred dollars a weekend to hear about her sense of things and LeeAnne believes that I should deal with issues that have baffled me since before the Fall of Rome. And to think that she started out wanting to teach second grade.

"There are half a dozen bills on my desk that are going to have to go out by the end of the week," I said. "The garden will need water, especially the jasmine and the snapdragons. That new bed that just looks like dirt is full of sweet peas and has to stay damp."

LeeAnne rolled her eyes. "I'll water the garden. Have I ever not watered the garden?"

"Well, there was that time right after Death Valley."

We smiled at each other, perhaps a little ruefully. On a trip to Death Valley, some nine years earlier, I had slept with Hannah for what turned out to be the last time, and upon finding out, LeeAnne had not only not watered the garden, she had doused it with gasoline and set fire to it. The poppies had burned with an unearthly beauty.

"I want to go to Nebraska too," Sammy stated suddenly, breaking his long silence.

LeeAnne looked alarmed and shot me a glance that said, *No way,* but I confess that something in me felt instantly it was the right thing to do. Out of the mouths of babes, and so forth. I don't think I liked the idea any more than LeeAnne did, though.

"I'll think about it," I told Sammy, in as discouraging a tone as possible, hoping that God or the Furies would contradict my initial reaction.

LeeAnne stood up abruptly and took her plate to the sink, where she began to wash it with a great deal of water. This clearly signified a Furies' vote. But she was going to let me handle it, because Hannah was Sammy's "real" mother after all and LeeAnne felt this wasn't her turf. Which was a crock of shit, frankly, but it is a crock of shit we have lived with for years, and natural enough given the situation.

Sammy, meanwhile, was still waiting, his energies gathered for a fight just as clearly as LeeAnne's. You can never tell where Sammy will take a stand, but once he takes one he is very tough to move. He looked a little like Gandhi, sitting there, ready to have his fuzzy little crew-cut head bashed in by British soldiers, perfectly resolute in his plain white pajamas, the only ones he will wear anymore. For some reason, a few months ago, small animals and airplanes and baseball players and all the other things that decorate kids' pajamas became unbearable to Sammy. He started sleeping in his junior BVDs and padding around the apartment during the pajama hours like a loinclothed prisoner on a hunger fast, his skinny ribs showing and his skin pale and chilled. It had taken a long search of practically every store in town to find some vanilla pj's bland enough for his iconoclasm. I was proud of what seemed a precocious integrity in him, but to tell you the truth I'd just as soon have Sammy contented with the Power Rangers and Barry Bonds, as the proper preparation for a normal, happy life.

And now he wanted to go to Nebraska. I glanced toward the sink, where LeeAnne continued to apply excessive water to the dishes. But LeeAnne was not going to help. Her back said only that this was mine to screw up, while the sight of her swelling belly, pressed against the edge of the counter, renewed my sense of the misery of life. The more formed and real that child grows within her, the more inescapably I am faced with my reluctant fatherhood.

"What time is the flight?" Sammy demanded.

"Seven," I replied, interested to see where he was going with it.

He checked his watch, then padded over to the telephone and dialed the time. In the Bay Area, you can do it by letters, P-O-P-C-O-R-N, and Sammy treats the service as a sort of oracle. He listened to the crisp, ever-wakeful voice announcing the ungodly hour, theatrically attentive; then he checked his watch again, also theatrically, and hung up.

"We've still got lots of time," he announced. "It's only 4:47."

I smiled in spite of myself, because he had me. Or God did. For good reasons or bad ones, I would take my son up the mountain and offer him to the awful truth. Somehow it just seemed like the thing to do.

"All right," I said resignedly. "All right."

"All *right*," Sammy crowed, as if he'd just scored from five yards out, which indicated to me that he really didn't have a clue.

At the sink, LeeAnne just scrubbed and scrubbed, though that plate must have been clean by then.

It may seem strange, in the light of Sammy and other evidence to the contrary, to insist that Hannah and I were not *about* sex. I would never be so foolish as to insist that sex had nothing to do with it at all. Sex had a lot to do with it. I was as wild for her as a man could be, and even now the images come easily enough of that particular curve of her breast, the line of her thigh from a private angle, the warm, slightly fuzzy cranny where her jawbone rounded at her neck. I can still smell her hair, willingly or unwillingly, still feel its tumbling weight surprising me, and I still recall the confidence of her hands, the frankness of her touch, the way the tips of her left hand's fingers—endearingly calloused from their endless fingering of the frets—made a slight dry rustling on my own thrilled skin. I can still make the blind pilgrimage in my mind at a moment's notice, tracing her vertebrae beneath the quilt on a winter Sunday morning, while dawn snow falls beyond the frozen window's glass.

And yet I can say honestly that for Hannah and me sex was really not the point. In the long run, my passion for her—and hers, perhaps, for me—only confused the issue. (Sammy being of course another, if obviously related, issue. But everything in its own time.)

After their squabble in the cafeteria that day, Hannah and Burton regrouped, and seemed to settle down a little. Hannah and I never spoke of our interlude in the snowy cemetery, but I could feel the quiet understanding between us after that.

Meanwhile, she had become part of our lives. We all

double-dated a few times, she and Burton, LeeAnne and I; we caught a movie or two, and played putt-putt golf. Hannah turned out to be a ferocious miniature golf player; refreshingly, she always played to win, while LeeAnne played to have a good time and Burton played as a commentary on the essential triviality of American leisure. I sweated every putt myself, and so it usually came down to the last hole between Hannah and me. More often than not she would bang some knee-shaking ten-footer in past the gorilla and through the legs of the giraffe to beat me by a stroke.

*"Pow!"* Hannah would exult as the putt dropped, punching the air as if she'd just won the U.S. Open. She even laughed with a Long Island accent.

After a period of cautious feline circling, it turned out that Hannah and LeeAnne actually liked each other, and for a while it seemed that they would bond over deep frank discussions of the flaws of their male companions and we would all settle into some kind of American sexual equilibrium. I remember several successful Friday nights when LeeAnne cooked a marvelous dinner featuring all the food groups—she has always been a willing and talented cook—and Hannah and Burton sparred in desultory fashion through the meal's two (or, on a particularly tricky evening, three) bottles of wine. Even LeeAnne would unbend to drink a glass or two, for sociability's sake, her cheeks taking on a warm, pink glow and her wit growing hilariously precise.

After dinner—and some persuasion—Hannah would bring out her guitar. Her transformation from a passionate, fun-loving, slightly contentious eighteen-year-old never failed to awe me. What *is* it in music that touches us so deeply? And what is in a voice? The warmth of Hannah's tones was like a promise realized, even then. Her picking style was still rudimentary; her lyrics would eventually embarrass her; her voice itself would grow much richer with the years. And yet my heart would open when she played. I would haul my sketchbook out and fill the pages, tracing Hannah in swirling, vertiginous strokes like a storm system on a weather map, unable quite to sort her out from the music; and, on the same page, I would draw Burton listening, cool and austere, and LeeAnne, her hair golden in the candlelight, the fine lines of her classic face simple and true.

LeeAnne, no fool, would cock an eyebrow at me, and I would nod back reassuringly. There seemed no contradiction possible, while the music played: no passions that could not be reconciled, no hurts that could not be healed, no sins that could not be forgiven. It seemed to me that our lives could unfold as Hannah's songs unfolded, from chord change to chord change, in seamless beauty.

After the musical interlude, LeeAnne would bring out coffee and dessert, and the four of us would play Scrabble. Our Scrabble games were intense, to be sure, riddled with kabbalistic chutes-and-ladders and subtextual mayhem, but what human activity isn't? In a manner of speaking we all became friends and might have survived indefinitely as people often do in even the trickiest of circumstances. LeeAnne and I would do the dishes together after Hannah and Burton had gone home, and I would treasure the quiet domesticity of the scene, the plates and saucers ordered in the drainer, the burned-down candles, the sensual dishevelment of LeeAnne's French braid, which unraveled just enough over the course of an evening to promise wildness later. If LeeAnne had met my eye and said, "You want to sleep with her," I would have denied it. It suited me to believe my sublimations were in place.

One day about a month after this soirée phase began, however, Hannah showed up at my studio. I was still working at that time out of the drafty old barn loft half a mile north of the cemetery. I paid an old farmer twenty-five dollars a month to let me share the place with six unproductive cows and a horse named Bessie. The smell of my oil paints and turpentine mingled with an atmosphere of decaying straw and dung from below and the occasional bovine ruckus, but I saw that as part of the alchemical work, the grounding of art in the most basic and literal shit. The farmer, a stolid old Mormon, had a profound mistrust of representational work and the deal was that I would not paint nudes, I suppose from fear of corrupting the cows. Nevertheless, it was a rule I would eventually break with Hannah.

It was a bleak afternoon in early November. I was working on a series of canvases based on the Zen ox-herding cycle at the time and was up to step three or four, as I recall, the ox's footprints in the mud. I'd recently fallen in love with the exquisite emptinesses of twelfth-century Chinese landscapes, but it was my intention to find that ox in an American terrain. As I labored to suggest (with suitable Sung understatement and a Utah accent) an overgrazed pasture after rain, I heard the cows downstairs stir. The stairs creaked and suddenly there was Hannah in a tremendous blue jacket with a fur-lined hood, carrying her guitar in its faded blue cloth bag.

"Hi," she said, with a shy glance at me. "I hope I'm not disturbing anything."

I shook my head mutely, lest I say something stupid. I was delighted to see her, frankly—wildly, inappropriately delighted. But I kept to the high ground of silence. Part of the advantage of being a painter is that people often expect you to be inarticulate. I have learned to hold my tongue and cover up a multitude of sins, at least temporarily.

"I was just feeling restless," Hannah went on. "I'm supposed to be studying for a biology exam." She set her guitar down and took off her coat, revealing the same sand-colored sweater she had worn to argue with Burton. She looked around for a moment, trying to find someplace to put the coat. But my studio lacked even the most rudimentary furniture and at last she gave up and laid it on the floor by the door.

"My God, what *is* that?" she exclaimed, noticing my canvas for the first time.

"Mud," I said proudly. I had begun much influenced by J.M.W. Turner and the songs of John Denver, and in my early days in Utah had painted landscape after saccharine Rocky Mountain landscape full of peaks and rainbows and cumulus clouds at sunset. But by the time Hannah showed up, I was into a winter palette purged of all but the bleakest grays and browns, feeling it was what the bombastic American soul required.

"Mud," Hannah repeated, unaccountably pleased. We stared

for a moment at the canvas. It was mud all right, and very understated. The ox was nowhere to be seen and even his footprints were a little smeary. But the mud was definitive.

Outside, the valley stretched north into the November haze, the mountains east and west receding into weak violet. At three in the afternoon the day's thin light already had the feeling of dusk.

"I hope you don't mind that I came over," Hannah said again, the first hint of insecurity I had ever heard from her. "I just needed someone to talk to."

The funny thing was, she did. And I did too. I still get dizzy thinking about how true it was, that need of hers to talk, and yet how deeply intermingled with the false.

"I'm glad you felt that you could talk to me," I said, with a perfectly straight face, as if I were a priest prepared to hear confession.

And so we talked. It was a simpler universe with which to be dissatisfied then and we made the most of our simpler alienation to build a spiritual rapport. Hannah was unhappy in school. Classes stifled real learning; the job market was not reality and preparation for the job market was not preparation for God and so on. Astonishingly, she and I shared a notion of the crucial centrality of preparation for God. She admired my lack of visible means of support—I was living like the lilies of the field.

Also, and also simplistically: Love with a biochemist was a baffling thing, not to mention love with a mime. Burton's view of the bleak abyss of secularity was too severe for Hannah. She didn't see how he could reconcile his X-ray vision of society's emptiness with an academic career (Burton was actually an excellent working scientist). We talked at length about the ins and outs of their obviously wrecked affair and I offered her enough hypocritical advice to raise the *Titanic*. We treated each other, perhaps a trifle too self-consciously, as high platonic colleagues, honoring absent lovers by keeping a three-foot space between our bodies at all times. But clearly we were doing the dance that leads to bed. Nothing fuels passion more than an attempted chastity, however feeble.

When we had run through one big round of talk, a natural pause occurred in which she might have gone back to her dorm and studied enough to pass the next day's biology test and possibly gone on to a responsible career in the world. But instead Hannah set up shop in the orange beanbag chair that served as my couch. She pulled her guitar from its cheap cloth case, tuning at some length to allow for the chilly room, running through a scale or two before slipping a capo onto the guitar neck. As she launched into a cover of Dylan's "Idiot Wind," complete with an authentic snarl, I started a kettle of water for tea on my little butane camper's stove. Then I fetched my sketchbook. The water took about half an hour to reach its boiling point on the feeble flame, and I must have done fifteen sketches of Hannah's hands before it did, certain that all the mystery of music was in them and that I was helping that mystery find its way onto the page for posterity. But frankly I had not even begun to learn how to work at my art then: It was all swift sketches and a few half-baked notions of Zen that made me feel so free. I was so smug and precious about it all that I can only shudder in retrospect—my little utopian world, far from the fray, sustained by the joy of art, a nascent sense of sacred reality, and all my unacknowledged lies. It was a bubble, but it was not inconsequential. God tempts us down our path with glimmers.

Still, I loved Hannah honestly enough, even then. Her voice was a miracle to me, making its warm inflections felt in a thousand surprising ways, and I could look at her face all day. There was two feet of old snow on the ground outside, and the wind whistled in around the edges of the skylight I had put in over the farmer's reservations. I was broke and foolish and had never sold a single work, but that was the winter of my contentment. In my mind I was still faithful to LeeAnne and I was Burton's true friend and I was a free man in my painting and in my understated Sung relations to the fallen world. My love for Hannah was as pure as her music. I could have died a happy idiot then and there, truly, and not have learned a thing.

When the tea was ready we did another round on her relationship to Burton and the rest of secular reality, to reassure us both that we were disinterested friends. Then we talked a great deal more about God and art and destiny. We both felt sure that God and art and destiny sufficed.

As night fell, the silences between us lengthened, and grew suggestive. We were both in the beanbag chair by now, our ritual gap down to about eight inches, ostensibly for warmth—my studio was heated only by a minuscule woodstove that didn't do the job. I had lit my kerosene lanterns and the world was a distant thing, beyond all the inward-reflecting windows.

At some point, with our faces just so and our souls aligned on God and art and destiny, I raised one hand to Hannah's cheek and kissed her. Chastely, the slightest brush of dry cool lips. And then again, more firmly. And then again, and her tongue flickered once, lightly, as our lips opened, and her left hand came up to my face and I felt for the first time the baffling density of her fingertips. I took her hand and kissed the callouses and it seemed to me I had never been more deeply appreciative of the beauty of a life consecrated to the highest things.

—

While LeeAnne helped Sammy pack—however much she might disapprove of him going to Nebraska, she was still determined to see that he took enough clean underwear—I slipped away to my studio. I had some vague idea of getting a few of my more accessible works out in the open, so that if my potential buyer decided to come by that afternoon anyway, LeeAnne could just walk him through the place and he'd be astounded by all the masterpieces leaning against the walls and leave a big check and an invitation to show in New York. But after sorting through a stack or two of paintings, it was clear to me that none of my works were accessible and that I had wasted my life. I was still painting mud. And Hannah was dead.

My work-in-progress sat on the easel, a study in earth tones and flame that wasn't sure yet if it was going to settle into a landscape or go up into abstract smoke. I'd been trying the night before to ground it with some heavy purple, but now it seemed to me that the purple was too obvious and too cautious. The only real thing on the canvas so far was the fire and I'd been afraid to let the fire have its way.

I reached for a tube of cadmium yellow, which burns about as hot as anything you could want, and squeezed it straight onto the canvas, then laid into the sloppy glob with a palette knife for texture. The purple, still wet itself, showed signs of life.

"Oh, Jerry, for God's sake..." LeeAnne exclaimed from the doorway, finding me at work.

"I know, I know. Is Sammy packed?"

"Oh yes."

Her tone said everything: *I have labored nobly in the service of a mistake.* "Look, I didn't pick this situation."

"Are you going to have him ID the body? 'Oh yes, Officer, that's Mommy all right.'"

"He calls her Hannah. And no, no, of course not."

"Then why take him at all?"

"He's going to have to deal with this for the rest of his life, no matter what," I said. "He might as well have something real to chew on. And he might as well know we did our best to face it together."

"And if he can't deal?"

Then he'll be just like Daddy, I thought. And God help us all. I wondered how LeeAnne would have advised one of her past-life clients to deal with this. But all they do is look back, of course; they are not so much focused on traumas-in-the-making. Usually they recall the sword that beheaded them, the battlefield on which they died, the taste of the flame that took their life, or the cell in which they wasted their productive years. They weep and shudder and occasionally scream, and presumably wake to their present life again renewed and freed of fear by some degree. No doubt some day Sammy himself would have to curl up on someone's therapeutic floor and recall an awful journey to a terrible place in the history of his soul. And would he blame me then? Or would he understand that I had been as helpless before the truth as he?

LeeAnne offered, more gently, "I packed you guys a lunch."

"Thanks," I said, moved; and then, on the strength of that, "It will be all right, sweetie."

"Will it now," LeeAnne murmured, her tone dry and flat, not buying it for a second. For all her New Age optimism, she really is a no-bullshit kind of gal. She turned to shuffle off down the hall. I stared at the canvas in front of me for a moment more, but I had no idea where to go with that yellow. It was just a big bright glaring smear of truth. I capped the tube of paint and laid a cloth over the canvas, then gathered myself to take a step, and then another step, and then another, into God-knows-what.

## four

# the fire and the wood

And Isaac spake unto Abraham his father, and said,
My father: and he said, Here am I, my son. And Isaac said,
Behold the fire and the wood: but where is the lamb
for the burnt offering?

And Abraham said, My son, God himself will provide
for the burnt offering: so they went,
both of them together.

Genesis 22:7–8

*At the airport,* LeeAnne kissed Sammy good-bye at
the curb, then handed him a snack in a bag for the airplane
ride. She had left the motor of our ancient blue Toyota running and was still so unhappy with me that it seemed for one
horrible moment she would just get into the car and drive
away. But at the last possible instant her arms opened up to me
and we embraced.

47

"Take care of him, for God's sake," she whispered fiercely in my ear. "Take care of *yourself.*"

"I will," I promised, conscious of the awkward angle our bodies made, the way we leaned into each other around the baffling bulk of the new life in her. It's going to be a girl, they tell us. I have even seen her already in the grainy sonograms, curled around the mystery of herself, formed knees bent as if in prayer, her folded hands against her face. LeeAnne insists she remembers the exact moment of conception, that she knew it when it happened: a Thursday afternoon in January, with a soft rain falling after a dry spell. A moment of sweetness.

While our bodies were pressed together, the baby kicked, and I felt the small sharp foot in my own belly.

"Say bye-bye to Daddy," LeeAnne said, pleased, seemingly without irony for the moment. She met my eyes as I leaned away, her gaze so full of animal innocence that it broke my heart.

On the plane, Sammy hopped into a starboard window seat, buckling his seatbelt with a bit of a self-conscious flourish before he settled back like the seasoned continental traveler he is. For the past two summers LeeAnne and I have put him on a plane in San Francisco and sent him off across the country to Hannah. She would meet him at Kennedy Airport and keep him for two weeks, teaching him Robert Johnson songs and undermining our hard-won position on the necessity of vegetables with dinner. The solo flights were a travel arrangement that nobody really liked but Sammy, who delighted in them, but it was the only way we had been able to figure out for Hannah to have some time with him. There was a big plane crash in all the headlines the week before the first trip we sent him on alone and I recall my sense of helplessness as I watched Sammy's plane taxi away from the gate. I spent the rest of the day hovering close to a radio, unable to get anything done, praying for mercy and listening for late-breaking news of another airline disaster. I didn't draw an easy breath until Sammy called collect from JFK, almost the minute he was on the ground, as I had insisted. I could hear Hannah in the background laughing and egging him on as he teased me about how easy it had been. But I know that Hannah sweated it too, every time he got on a plane. If only she had sweated her own journeys half as much.

As the plane taxied into position for takeoff through a thin but still unnerving fog, Sammy unzipped his little carry-on bag, custom-made by LeeAnne, and took out his battery-powered portable synthesizer keyboard, complete with headphones. This expensive little item has been his constant companion since Hannah gave it to him for his sixth birthday a couple years ago. Sammy went more or less straight from "Twinkle, Twinkle, Little Star" on a five-key plastic xylophone to playing Bach and scathing Delta blues on an instrument that could create the orchestral soundtrack for a feature film. Frankly, he is a bit of a prodigy, and it terrifies me. What gave me joy in Hannah lives in Sam as well, but I am quite sure that it is precisely what gave me joy in Hannah that has burnt my own life black as a scrap of gristle on an open flame, and that killed her young.

Paradoxically, it is LeeAnne who has insisted on Sammy's twice-a-week piano lessons. She encourages him in his music, listening and applauding and getting it all on tape, while I am constantly trying to get him out in the backyard to play catch with whatever ball is in season, and to edge him deeper into Little League baseball, where he is a passable shortstop with a good arm and a promising stroke at the plate. Music means something different to LeeAnne. It is a hearth flame that warms, and not a forest fire. She has a very healthy view of art.

Also—there is no escaping it—LeeAnne wants to avoid any suspicion of seeming to quash the Hannah strain in Sammy. There is true nobility in this, but I think that sometimes she leans too far in the other direction. There has never been a real question of suppressing Hannah's presence in Sammy. From the start, Hannah-in-Sammy has been perfectly robust, and even blatant. Hannah-in-Sammy screamed and wailed and threw things, and crapped in its bed. It puked and drooled and ran a fever and broke anything it could reach. Not to overemphasize the uncharming aspects of it all, but Hannah-in-Sammy could be a big loud unavoidable pain in the butt, and LeeAnne never needed to pay any extra dues in my eyes. She has raised the kid as her own, with unflinching love; she has nurtured him body and soul and never squeaked a single complaint. It is more than I could ever have dared to ask.

The plane roared down the runway and lifted into the sky. Sammy pressed his face to the window, alive with a child's awe at the miracle of flight. I leaned over him to look too. We banked right over the Bay, climbing steadily, and suddenly the plane burst free of the clouds. Across an ocean of impenetrable cotton-white, the sun was coming up. Sammy reached for my hand, acknowledging the beauty of it, while I sat beside him trying not to cry.

After a while he let go of my hand, put his headphones on, and concentrated on his keyboard again, his hand movements heedless and free, although all I could hear was the clicking of the keys. Sometimes I'll hear that clicking at night from behind the closed door of his bedroom, and if I ease the door open and look in, all I'll see is the tentlike peak of his blanket, while Sammy plays under the covers in secret.

The stewardess paused beside us, amused and impressed by Sammy's absorption.

"He has your hair," she noted.

I hesitated, then smiled. Really, we can't spend our whole lives explaining our pain to strangers.

"And his mother's eyes," I replied.

The day after my makeout session with Hannah in the barn studio, I tried to make a gentle confession to LeeAnne, focusing as much as possible on the extended discussions of God and art and destiny and minimizing the activity in the beanbag chair. But there was no way around the mammalian bottom line. LeeAnne reacted to the news with heartfelt simplicity, throwing every single item of mine in her possession out the bedroom window into the snow. I realized that for an itinerant Zen artist living like the lilies of the field, I had accumulated an awful lot of shoes and shirts and underwear in her closet.

LeeAnne's roommates helped her gleefully, stripping watercolors and sketches I had given her from the apartment walls. These sailed out into the snow as well, where I scrambled to retrieve them before they got too wet. Once I went outside after one of the watercolors, LeeAnne would not let me back in: My coat and boots sailed out shortly afterward, followed by three oranges, a can of soup, and half a loaf of bread, representing her scrupulous sense of the grocery division.

The roommates thought my betrayal of LeeAnne would drive her back into the arms of the Mormon church. She had been skimping on attendance at her local ward's services since getting involved with me. But there was already no going back to the Mormon religion for LeeAnne. Still in the throes of the stimulus-response paradigm, her reading of the betrayal was primarily psychological: Like the rat that I was, I had succumbed to a conditioned response. Also, more romantically, artists were not to be trusted. This reinforced LeeAnne's original intention to marry someone who had stayed in school.

"I still love you," I told her from below the window, my wardrobe and a host of sentimental items scattered in the snow around me like the feathers of a sparrow caught by a cat. "This doesn't need to change anything between *us.*"

"Oh fuck off, Jerry," LeeAnne said. "I could see this coming from a hundred miles off." And then she slammed the window shut. I had to admire her style, frankly, even then. LeeAnne really had much too great a sense of her own dignity to be a Skinnerian for long.

The next day I gathered my courage for what I feared would be a similar encounter with Burton. The two of us played raquetball together every Thursday and I was wary and guilt-ridden as I laced up my tennis shoes. Burton for some time now had been using the protracted death of his sexual relationship with Hannah to make the case for celibacy, but I doubted his sincerity. He said he found Hannah unreasonable, which of course she was, but "fascinating." This fascination was the source of all suffering in the world, according to Burton. And so forth: a surprisingly orthodox interpretation of Genesis. We battered the little blue ball off all four walls and the ceiling, making up our own rules as we went, as we always did. Between points we talked in our usual ambling way. I was looking for a painless opening to break the news, but after the incident with LeeAnne I was gun-shy.

"Hannah thinks the mime troupe should be more politically active," Burton told me.

"Well?" I served. Burton returned halfheartedly and I put him away with a ruthless shot into the corner. Hannah's unreasonable fascination was definitely affecting his game, while guilt and the burden of betrayal appeared to be improving mine.

"Well, what use is politics when the body is riddled with cliché?"

I smiled. Hannah would have had me harping on our civilization's sad state as well: the imminence of catastrophe, the palpable approach of doom, the necessity of taking painting to the streets. Stymied in her biology class, afraid to put too much weight on music, she was toying with finding some crucial relevance in the voting behavior of large numbers of people. But at the ripe old age of twenty I was easy with the notion that civilizations come and go. Like Burton's grandfather, I had my eye on the bigger dot of oblivion. And if it was all going down the drain, I wanted to get my burnt umber right.

I served again. Burton hit another fat return and I pulverized it out of reach. My game was embarrassingly sharp, even as my mind ransacked its storehouse of self-justifying truisms. Had I stolen Hannah, fascination and all, or had Burton lost her? Such were the puny terms that preoccupied me. God, art, and destiny had led me inexorably into soap opera.

"Burton, there's something I have to tell you," I said at last.

Burton glanced at me in his cool and easy way. "I already know."

"You—already know?"

"LeeAnne called me last night. She's really rather angry with you. But handling it well, I think."

I stood for a long moment with my racket dangling on its wrist strap, trying to fathom a consciousness that could have let me twist and squirm through most of a best-of-five-games set of raquetball without even a wink toward the unmentionable. But that was Burton: a genuinely surprising soul.

"Let's make anything that lands behind this line a wild card ball," Burton said, while I pondered and floundered and sought new terms.

I stirred. "A wild card ball?"

"A wild card ball changes the field of play," Burton explained patiently. I had seen him with his mime troupe just so, explaining that a precise arbitrary posture could baffle years of automatism. "Scoring becomes optional and you can let it bounce twice. Or even three times. Two bounces doubles the point value and three bounces—"

"Triples it?"

"Multiplies it by four," Burton said, with a trace of superiority. "The progression is geometric. Also, see that square?"

"Yes."

"If you hit that square, all scores go back to zero."

I hesitated, dubious, then shrugged. "Let's try it."

I served, the ball landing just beyond the line in question. Burton let it bounce twice, then jumped on the wild card ball like a cat and smacked it neatly into the center of the square.

"Zero–zero," he smiled. "My serve."

It was a Burton classic, I suppose: less forgiveness than a simple rejection of the expected script of blame. I knew then that I had blown any chance I'd ever had of knowing what he really felt.

And so, reduced to situation comedy in my deepest relationships, I went on. Hannah came by the barn studio that same night. It turned out that she had dropped out of school while I was suffering my revelations with LeeAnne and Burton, completing the paperwork to blow her scholarship with an efficiency she had never shown while studying for biology tests. We really had not gone so many steps across our bridge to justify burning it so completely. But the greater part of experience is acquired in sink-or-swim situations. If we were smart, we would never grow wise.

Hannah came up the steps with her guitar, and some toiletries and two changes of clothes in a day pack, wearing her comic blueberry parka over that same sand-colored sweater, and a modified Yankees cap with ear flaps. The cows downstairs lowed uneasily, not used to so much activity after dark. On the easel, my work-in-progress was a thicket and a glimpse of the ox's ass. A single kerosene lamp burned in the window, and the studio's small woodstove warmed the air in a six-inch radius from the center of the room. We never did get running water in that place; it was as primitive as our notions of divinity.

Hannah paused one step inside the door, hopeful and uncertain and afraid she had presumed. She seemed childlike in that Yankees cap, her young cheeks red with the cold. I met her eyes from across the room, feeling solemn and giddy and shamefully aware that the sight of her eased the sense of a hole torn in me that I had lived with in the days since LeeAnne began throwing my socks and charcoal sketches into the snow. I had no sense of replacing one woman with another. LeeAnne was irreplaceable; I had not intended to lose her in the first place; and in any case Hannah would tear a different kind of hole soon enough. I think I knew that, even then. But it was good to see her. There was always great comfort for me in Hannah's face.

I crossed to meet her and slipped between the flaps of her open parka to put my arms around her waist.

"If I can't sleep here, I'm sleeping with the cows," Hannah

said, perhaps a little defensively. "I'm sure as hell not going *back.*"

"Of course you're not," I said. "Of course you're staying here."

She relaxed perceptibly; apparently she really hadn't known what I would say. Brave soul, to have launched herself into the abyss with so little certainty of shelter. I took the navy-blue Yankees cap off her head and kissed her heavy dark hair as it fell free. I kissed her temple, her forehead, her cheek and her nose, awash in the baffling new scent of her, until her lips found mine. Our hands began to move, finding layers and easing into depths. Hannah's waist beneath the heavy sweater was slimmer than I would have imagined; a whole surprisingly slim body lived beneath that mass of wool. There was still so much that we had to learn about each other.

We began, like the near-children we were, with sex, and it is astounding to me, looking back, that the relationship did not founder there. I had been a virgin with LeeAnne, and she with me, and we had eased into sex together like Catholic high school sweethearts, by a series of minute gradations that each seemed daring, over a period of months. It was the endless foreplay of the inexperienced and the nearly chaste, an exquisite thing indeed: I knew every button in LeeAnne's wardrobe long before I knew her skin and I came to know her beloved body inch by gradual inch, finding my way by tongue and touch like a sandpiper, working the edge of her slow-retreating tide of clothes.

With Hannah, on the other hand, there was no comforting shore from which to ease into the water; we were at sea in a single night. I wanted her, wildly, but I was painfully conscious of the fact that she was not LeeAnne. Had I been an older man—had I been the man I am now, I suppose—my guilt might have made me impotent and forced us into fruitful conversation, but youth prevailed over conscience and I was merely terrified, hasty, heated and heedless. I came almost immediately and was sure the deal was off. But Hannah was tender with me, very patient. She had seen worse than me in high school, as it turned out; two years younger than me, she was much more seasoned, and inclined to forgive.

We lay quietly on the lumpy floor-level mattress that served as my studio's bed, our arms around each other, and slowly my panic subsided. The moisture on the inside of the nearest window had frozen already and through the smooth sheet of ice the night sky was filled with slightly distorted stars. We talked about the future: how we would live pure, free lives and do our art. How we would be fearless.

"I already know how I'm going to die," Hannah told me.

Maybe I should have tried harder to talk her out of it, right from the start. Maybe what she was begging for was a little perspective and some common sense. But I'm not sure she would have been in bed with me at that point, if what she'd been looking for was common sense. I just laughed and said, "Don't be silly. You're going to live forever." We reached for each other again, more tenderly this time, and the second time we began to get it right.

While we waited for our connecting flight in the Houston airport, Sammy went into one of the little airport shops filled with overpriced picante sauce and keychains shaped like the Alamo, to buy a map of Nebraska. The woman behind the counter shook her head—all they had was the greater Houston area and the Lone Star State Self-Guided Tour. They really didn't get much call hereabouts for maps of Nebraska, she told Sammy, winking over his head at me at what a businesslike little guy he was. Oklahoma, now, that was a different story.

Sammy thanked her politely and turned away. Three steps from the counter he began to cry. Shoulders heaving, face contorted, but completely silent: Sammy would have choked before emitting an audible sob in public. I got him out of the stream of traffic and held him close, feeling the wet heat of his face through my shirt, heart-high as I bent to him, feeling the shuddering of his fragile body as a pain in my own. And thinking, automatically: *LeeAnne was right, of course, I should never have brought him here.* But the truth was, I really couldn't think of any place on the planet now where Sammy wouldn't cry. So I was glad he was with me.

## five

## this side of golden

Go forward, knowing the Path will vanish under you
Open your arms, knowing they will burn away
Give everything you are, knowing it is nothing
Bathe always in His river, even when it's blood.

Rumi

---

**On the ground in Omaha,** the first thing we did was buy a map. I spread it over a table in the airport coffee shop and Sammy and I leaned over it like pirates looking for an X. According to Officer Barnes's laconic instructions, our route lay southwest: a little town called Golden, ten miles beyond Papillion, across the Platte River. If we got to Waverly, the policeman had told me, we'd gone too far. Apparently you could miss Golden, if you blinked. Hannah herself had been on her way to Lincoln.

"Here's where we are," I told Sammy, pointing to Omaha on the map. "And here's the town where we're going."

"And that's where Hannah died?"

"Somewhere east of there, I think."

Sammy studied the map intently. He had cried more on the flight from Houston to Omaha but he was calm now, all business. It was just after noon in our new time zone and he had already reset his watch scrupulously to Central Time; now he was looking for a handle on space as well. *Here we were, and here Hannah had died, and here was the road between the two.* The map was not the territory but, obviously, the map was very important.

At last Sammy looked up at me. "Okay."

"Okay," I said. "Let's go rent the car." I reached for the map but Sammy was already trying to fold it up. It took him quite a while to get it down to a manageable size, but I let him figure it out himself. The exercise seemed to comfort him, and in any case it didn't seem to me that we were in a hurry. There was nothing in Nebraska but grief for us, as far as I was concerned, and I knew the way to that by heart.

We took I-80 west out of Omaha in our rented Ford, a jaunty red Escort. Sammy commented several times on the new-car smell. I realized that this was probably the first time in his life he had been in a car with less than 120,000 miles on it. One more side effect of being raised by a painter and a past-life specialist.

We crossed the Platte River bridge and got off the interstate at the Ashland exit, heading west on an unassuming, ruler-straight two-lane road. They'd told us in Omaha we could expect thunderstorms in the afternoon, but this seemed impossible. The featureless land baked in the late August sun beneath a vast blue sky without a cloud. Sammy kept fiddling with the Escort's air conditioning and the radio, as much for the novelty as for the need. There were still a few stands of tall ripe corn left here and there, but most of the fields had been harvested and the dry stubble gave the land a ravaged look. There was almost no traffic on the road, only the occasional pickup truck, the drivers' heads swiveling at our alien red Ford.

On such a road you could see things a long way off, and so I saw the cluster of vehicles at an accident site from almost a mile away, long before I realized that we'd come upon the place where Hannah had died.

—

I don't know if I changed Hannah's life. Hannah herself was not a person who thought in those terms—she thought of herself as someone on a mission from God, to steal a phrase from the *Blues Brothers,* and she had a strong sense of fate. In her view, we had not affected each other so much as we had recognized each other: We were players in the same drama. In another time and place she might have been a wild-haired prophet or a heroine out of Aeschylus or Shakespeare, but we were American children, white kids from the suburbs of Long Island and Virginia. Hannah was supposed to go to Juilliard and learn classical guitar and I had been slated for Stanford as an idiot savant in math, but we had both found our way to Utah, into the desert and the mountains, avoiding the coasts by a weird, half-blind instinct. A hundred miles south of us, a hundred years before, the first Mormon settlers had dug in in the wilderness, looking to cultivate a new relationship with God.

A century later, Hannah and I dug in too, in the loft of the barn of one of their descendants, to cultivate God knows what.

When I think back on the winter that Hannah and I spent in that primitive barn loft, even now, through a sobering haze of years, I see everything in a clear winter light so full of joy I almost despair of even hinting at it. And yet if I ignore that joy, nothing that followed makes any sense. My life turned on that fleeting joy like a door opening easily on a hinge.

It was strange at first to have her there in the studio—like having someone else in your dream. I had been there with the cows for almost a year by then and had tasted something of the essential loneliness of the working artist, and I suspected that I was already too far gone to share the view. LeeAnne had always avoided my studio; she found it uncongenial and uninhabitable. But Hannah was oddly at home in that spare, strange place. It wasn't that she put up curtains —she was not the curtain-putting-up sort. But she made it seem possible to live there at all, by taking the third-world conditions of our little garret in stride. She was out of bed early her first morning there, building a fire in the stove, heating water for coffee, putting on layer after layer of clothing and walking around the room wrapped in a blanket like a Hollywood Indian squaw, laughing out loud at the glamorous absurdity of it all, her laughter making big breath-clouds in the frosty air. Hannah had a marvelous laugh, large, easy, and forgiving.

I spent a lot of time in those days just sketching her, while she sat by the window where the light was best, playing the guitar. The studio's single stool rocked slightly, but Hannah could actually keep its unsteadiness on beat, so that the click-click-click of the uneven legs served as a kind of percussion section. Hannah would strum away—she was writing a lot of songs about the road then, though she had never really been on the road. Her face was endless to me. I could see everything there—courage and clarity, innocence and grit, truth and laughter and sorrow and terror and beauty. Sometimes I would pass into a sort of ecstasy and just sit there and look at her, marveling; and sometimes Hannah would catch me at this and laugh. She generally found me ridiculous, in a lovable way. I *was* ridiculous, of course. Yet Hannah confirmed my calling to the even deeper ridiculousness of art, just by being there, just by being who she was. At a point in my young life when I might finally have begun to wonder at the thinness of the limb I had climbed out on, Hannah showed up and urged me on. She believed in me, oddest of all; and I believed in her. We were each other's first audience and first peers.

It's not that there was a shortage of reality checks. The walk to the outhouse itself, a brutal pilgrimage over frozen ground with the wind coming out of the canyon mouth like a knife blade, would have sobered a Sufi. Hannah had to cut the fingers out of some gloves to practice the guitar; I had to cut up another pair of gloves to hold a pencil while I sketched. We showered in the locker rooms at the university gym, and when the gym was closed we did not shower. We ate an unconscionable amount of crackers and cheese. We had no money, no electricity, no furniture, no running water, and no prospects. The stove smoked and the water bowl froze and the whole place stank of cows.

Burton had already regrouped, post-Hannah, doubling his course load to pursue an early degree. LeeAnne's new boyfriend, acquired a little defiantly within a week of the fiasco with me, was a returned Mormon missionary majoring in political science, on a law school track. While the rest of the world raced on into normality, Hannah and I meandered into a lovely nowhere. We were bent on living on our art, but our art at that point, frankly, was no great shakes. All we had was legs for a leap of faith.

The thing is, everything was beautiful. I'd rather bite my tongue off than have to say it so stupidly and so inadequately. Beauty everywhere my eye saw light, a richness of such wild, unlikely specificity that the most ordinary sights became delight. Every object seemed to be lit quietly from within, and every new moment brought a beautiful surprise—barn dust making its gentle whirl through a shaft of sunlight late in the afternoon, an old hammer rusting on a cobwebbed shelf, or the bleak blue mountains just before new snow. No poetry suffices to describe what I am talking about. But a man must speak, if only to babble in awe.

Given the wintry conditions, Hannah and I spent as much of our nonartistic time as possible in bed, where a stack of blankets from the local Mormon equivalent of the Salvation Army created a haven of warmth. But our sex life was surprisingly hit-or-miss. We both were creatures of moodiness and whim, high-strung and prone to slipping out of tune. When conditions were right, we would make love for hours at a time, a slow dance of passion, our every movement measured and focused by the weight of the blankets and the need to keep the heat sealed in beneath them. Hannah's hands were intelligent, knowing and sure, and her responsive flesh was smooth and firm. I loved the low timbre of her moan. Her body was like a foreign city to me, beloved but never wholly known, rich and intricate and full of unexpected sensitivities, little cul-de-sacs of delight and sudden vistas of ecstasy. Returning to my painting after such lovemaking, the canvas itself would seem like a continuation of Hannah's flesh, alive to every feather-stroke, surrendering color along the nerves of its images like heat, like shudders of pleasure.

At other times, though, Hannah and I would find ourselves baffled in the simplest mundane exchanges, prickly with each other and out of sync. It is a danger, I suppose, of relying too much on magic: An ordinary day at less than fever pitch came to seem like a sort of failure. We grew superstitious, attributing the eclipses of passion to the moon and stars, to subtleties of karma and minute fluctuations in the practice of our art, but I suspect now that part of our problem was all the things we weren't talking about. A number of topics were taboo, including realistic economics. But foremost among the forbidden subjects was LeeAnne.

I had seen LeeAnne only once since Hannah had moved into the barn loft. We met one afternoon in December for her to return a few of my things that she had failed to throw out into the snow, including a big, lush book of reproductions of Vermeer.

"Oh, no, not the Vermeer," I exclaimed. "You should keep that. We bought it together."

"Exactly," LeeAnne replied, merciless and succinct, and placed the heavy volume in my hands, along with my old toothbrush, a refrigerator magnet—a little plastic solar face I had given her once upon a time, that said, "You are my sunshine"—and a pair of old tennis shoes without laces.

LeeAnne, disencumbered, brushed her hands together briskly. "I took back your library books, by the way—they were overdue. You owe me $4.38."

I had a five in my limp wallet, which I had been saving up for a tube of cerulean blue paint. My skies lately, it seemed to me, had lacked a certain quality. But I dug the bill out promptly and handed it over. LeeAnne made scrupulous change, handing me back exactly sixty-two cents.

"So how've you been?" I said, trying to prolong the moment.

LeeAnne smiled. "Ah, Jerry. You perfect, fucking prick." And she walked away.

I stood for a moment in the winter twilight, watching her go, reminding myself I had no right to be sentimental. But her giving the Vermeer back hurt. We had shared a love for his luminous ordinary scenes, leafing through the book together by the hour, treasuring the daily moments lit with quiet radiance: the sunlight on a purple velvet chairback, or a pearl button's iridescent sheen.

At last I made the long walk home to the studio. Hannah,

thoughtfully, had the stove fired up when I got there, and the loft was as warm as it would ever be that winter. She was sitting near the fire as I came in, playing something that sounded like sunny weather. She gave me a smile that said she was on a roll and I nodded to her to keep going. Setting my sad pile of returned goods aside without comment, I began assembling our usual supper of crackers, cheese, canned oysters, and the cheapest wine. By candlelight, I couldn't help but think, the little feast on that rickety table looked like something out of Vermeer, if I'd only had the chops to paint it.

It couldn't last, and it didn't. It didn't even last until spring. Hannah's father came out to Utah in early March. As it turned out, she hadn't told her family that she had dropped out of school: one more of our unexamined topics. But George Johnson had called her dorm and somehow coaxed the fact from her former roommate, and he had taken the next plane to Salt Lake and rented a car to drive north. Hannah went into a tizzy from the moment she learned that he was in town, and it was at that point that I began to realize how flimsy our little bubble of beauty and joy really was. Her panic was genuine and very deep. Apparently she could handle the thought of dying in a car wreck like it was an old friend; and she could face the future without plumbing, heat, or a reliable source of income; but she couldn't face her father.

To compound the situation, it was Burton who delivered the news. The old roommate had given Burton's phone number to Hannah's father for some reason, and the first thing

George Johnson had done was call Burton and threaten to horsewhip him. This delighted Burton, who came out to the barn to tell us all about it.

"Did he actually say that?" I asked him. "'Horsewhip'?"

"That very word."

"He's been threatening to horsewhip every boyfriend I've had since the sixth grade," Hannah said disgustedly. Clad in the usual two pairs of socks, long johns and sweatpants, doubled sweaters and woolen cap that was our artistic lounging attire that winter, she had been circling the loft like a fat moth in a jar since Burton had arrived with the news.

"Great," I groaned. "Horsewhipped."

"Oh don't worry, he'd never do it. He's too good a lawyer to risk getting sued." Hannah shook her head. "Damn him! How could he just show *up* like this?"

She was actually pouty about it, I noted with amazement. I generally thought of Hannah as being about ten thousand years old, if not timeless. It was difficult to reconcile my *anima* image of her with that protruding lower lip.

"He's very upset that you dropped out of school," Burton said. "He wanted to know if you were pregnant and, if so, what my intentions were. It was thrilling, actually."

"What did you *say?*"

"I told him that I certainly intended to remain Hannah's friend no matter what her condition was. I think he began to realize at that point that he had the wrong cad."

I laughed, but Hannah didn't even smile.

"Where is he staying?" she asked Burton grimly.

"The American Hotel, in town."

"Of course. Nothing but the best for George T. Johnson, Esquire."

I laughed again, because the American Hotel was hardly the Ritz-Carlton. It was a decent little place on Main Street, where the governor of Utah had stayed once in 1947. But Hannah's sense of humor was long gone. She glared at me and demanded, "What's so funny?"

"Nothing," I said, unwilling to fight about it.

Burton's right eyebrow cocked upward slightly, registering the exchange. But he was entitled, I suppose, to take what small pleasure he could in me finding Hannah difficult at last.

—

Only when we got close did it really register: a lane full of burning flares, a scatter of glass on the roadway, two Nebraska Highway Patrol cars, and a tow truck trying to winch a pale green Chevy van out of the ditch alongside yet another field of corn stubble. I would have thought they'd have had it all cleaned up by now, but apparently the vehicle wedged into the ditch had proven recalcitrant. I had last seen that van in Hannah's driveway in Connecticut, two months before, the day before the Blue Flame Band's tour had begun. It looked like a wrecked accordion now, crumpled, skewed, and scorched. I slowed, helplessly, then stopped. Beside me, Sammy's eyes were wide.

"Stay here," I told him, and got out of the car. It was like stepping into a furnace; I was sweating before I'd taken a step. In the hot air everything seemed lazy and dreamlike. A flock

of crows scavenging in the disheveled field took off as my car
door slammed, black on bleached gold. I thought of Van Gogh,
involuntarily—the late paintings, that mad hallucinogenic clarity. In the heat and misery, my eye was very sharp. I walked
slowly toward the two policemen, who were standing beneath
a yellow crossroads sign watching the tow truck driver down
in the ditch. They both eyed me unencouragingly as I walked
up. Beneath my feet glass crunched on the gray asphalt.

"Nothing to see here, sir," one of the cops said brusquely.
"Nothing to be done. Best to just keep the traffic moving."

"My friend was in the van."

They both looked troubled for a moment, almost comical
twin shadows passing across their strong grim faces. Then the
second one said, more gently, "We're sorry, sir. But there still
ain't nothing to be done."

"I suppose there's not." But something in me was not yet
ready to go and I held my ground. The two policemen looked
at me.

"Are either of you Barnes?" I asked. They looked blank. "I
talked to an Officer Barnes, on the phone, this morning."

"Oh, Lamar, sure," the second cop said. "I guess he was handling the notifications."

"He said he'd be in Golden."

"That's five miles up the road or so. There's a county hospital there, the third right after you come into town. I imagine
he's still dealing with the paperwork."

I nodded, but still made no move to go. In the roadway, the
burning flares gave off a low hissing sound, like incandescent

snakes. The crows had circled and settled in the field again. In the ditch, the tow truck driver was quietly swearing to himself, trying to get a cable looped on the van. The two cops looked a little amused, in spite of themselves.

I said, looking along the highway, "I don't see any skid marks."

The cops glanced at each other.

"Weren't any skid marks in this one," the second cop answered. "It happened too fast. Nobody ever touched the brakes."

"Is that unusual?"

He shrugged uneasily. "We figure the driver fell asleep."

I could see Sammy in the car, his face pale through the windshield. It still didn't seem to me that Hannah would have fallen asleep. She wasn't the sleepy type. "Yeah . . . Well, I'd better get going, I guess."

"Sorry about your friend," the first cop said.

I looked at him, not wanting to answer, because somehow it seemed like losing that much more of Hannah, to act like those words had meaning. But the man meant well. I nodded, and walked away.

In the car, the air conditioning turned my skin clammy. My shirt was soaked through. Sammy studied my face, looking for cues.

"Is this where Hannah died?" he asked.

I looked at the flares sizzling in the road, thinking that you could never paint that live pink-white magnesium gleam. It wasn't even a color, it was just naked light. It was a kind of blindness.

"Yes, it is," I told him. "So it's a good place to pray for her."

We bowed our heads. It even seemed that Sammy took some comfort in it. But I couldn't really pray for Hannah yet. If she'd been driving, I was mad at her; and if she hadn't, I was mad at God.

## into the noon

It is to be learned—
This cleaving and this burning,
But only by one who
Spends out himself again.

Then, drop by caustic drop, a perfect cry
Shall string some constant harmony,—
Relentless caper for all those who step
The legend of their youth into the noon.

Hart Crane, "Legend"

**Golden, Nebraska,** population 1,800, was announced by a big yellow sign adorned with the insignia of the Elks and the Moose Lodge and the Kiwanis and the Knights of Columbus. The town seemed at first to be nothing but a change in the speed limit signs from 55 to 35. But over a slight rise there were trees and houses, gas stations, a Kmart, and several plain little clapboard churches. The county hospital signs were prominent along Main Street and we found the place easily at the third right turn: a modest two-story building of rusty brick that might have passed for a schoolhouse.

The sleepy parking lot was three-quarters empty in the midday sun. Sammy and I walked somberly through ripples of heat into the cool vestibule. I set him up in the waiting area with his keyboard and his copy of *Harriet the Spy*. We had talked about this part of the trip, on the plane and again in the car on the way here. It was a job that had to be done, a formality, part of our mission to do right by Hannah and take her home to Long Island.

"Are you going to be okay here for a while?" I asked, a little uneasily.

Sammy nodded. He seemed oddly cheerful, which baffled me.

"I don't know how long this will take. It looks like there are some soda machines down the hall, if you want anything. You've got some quarters, right?"

Sammy nodded again.

"Okay," I said. I hesitated for a moment, feeling utterly lame, then kissed his forehead and turned to go.

"If it's not Hannah, can we just go home?" Sammy blurted.

I hesitated, ambushed by the cruel flimsiness of that sudden secret child's hope. But this was not the place to fight for truth.

"Of course," I told him. I kissed him again, and crossed the lobby to the desk. The slick stone floor had recently been waxed and I walked gingerly, sure that anyone who looked at me would call immediately for a doctor. It seemed to me that

I had been torn open right across my chest and was spilling my insides onto that treacherous floor with every step. But the perky nurse behind the desk just smiled at me, pleasantly enough, and asked in perfect flat Nebraska English how she could be of help.

—

In the end, Hannah and I went into town to meet the dragon. Hannah assured me that her father would have had the police find us, otherwise. When I met George Johnson I realized that this was probably true. A former assistant DA in New York City, now involved in a lucrative private practice, Johnson was clearly a man who was used to having his own way, a wielder of casual authority. He was not a large man, but he was solid, even meaty, and his energy was large; added to his square shoulders and paunch it was enough to make him an imposing presence. His hair was a suspiciously vivid shade of black for a man in his early fifties, but he lived up to it well enough. Certain people earn their small conceits through incessant labor and there was never any doubt in my mind that George Johnson had paid his dues.

Hannah and I had agreed to meet him for dinner in the homely little restaurant associated with the American Hotel and he was already seated at a table for three as we walked into the dining room, his thousand-dollar suit standing out from the local meatloaf dinner crowd like an elk's antlers in a dairy herd. He rose as we approached and moved to kiss his daughter's cheek, but Hannah baffled him by leaning away, offering a cool handshake instead. She still had her grim face on, but

George Johnson ignored this, more or less. He seemed genuinely glad to see her, and was willing to suffer certain indignities for the privilege.

"You look wonderful, darling," he boomed, but Hannah
wasn't having any of it.

"Dad, this is Jeremiah Mason," she said curtly. "Jeremiah, my
father."

I held out my hand. "Mr. Johnson."

"Jeremiah," her father said formally, eyeing me. As a result of
this slightly perverse introduction of Hannah's, he would call
me Jeremiah for the next twenty years. Still, he was committed to heartiness; he seized my hand and pumped it furiously.
The energy of a sublimated horsewhipping, I thought, or perhaps I simply had not had enough experience with a successful American grip. In any case, I felt quite wrung. I was looking
for Hannah in his face, but finding nothing of her there.
George Johnson's jaw was strong as a pit bull's where Hannah's
was delicate, his nose was heavier and slightly blunt and would
not have been out of place in a boxing ring, and his eyes, far
from her turbulent indigo, were the kindly blue of a sky without weather.

We sat down. The waiter came by with menus; Hannah's
father asked for the wine list and learned that there wasn't a
wine list. There wasn't even a beer list. There was a soft drink
list. We all dutifully ordered Coca-Cola with our meals.

"Can you believe this place?" George Johnson marveled,
shaking his head as the waiter walked away. "There isn't any
liquor in the whole damned state, as far as I can tell. Hell, with
this bleak landscape, you'd think they'd be grateful for a little

relief, but I suppose you've got to deal with the religious element. . . . Fortunately—" He glanced left and right, like a high school kid about to take a drag on a cigarette, then reached for the briefcase at his feet and came up with a fifth of Scotch. "I have not come unprepared."

"For God's sake, Daddy," Hannah exclaimed disgustedly.

"Nonsense, this is purely social, purely social," Johnson insisted, pouring a double shot into his water. "Hannah? Jeremiah?"

Hannah shook her head. But I said, "Maybe a drop. In a purely social sense."

Johnson smiled delightedly. "That's the spirit!" He leaned across the table and the Scotch went glug-glug-glug, a strong inducement to sociability that turned my water the color of ginger ale.

A kindly, stout middle-aged woman in a cotton flower-print dress at the next table had noticed the proceedings and was clearly trying to decide whether to complain to someone or not. Living in Utah was in many ways like living in Prohibition times, except that alcohol was harder to come by. But Hannah's father met the woman's eye and winked, deftly. The woman colored a faint, pleased pink. She smoothed her dress, then turned her attention back to her meatloaf and peas.

I was impressed. Anyone who could charm a Mormon farmer's wife with an illegal bottle of Scotch in his hand was a man to be reckoned with.

Our food arrived. The meal passed laboriously, barely kept in motion by George Johnson's devastating critique of the American Hotel Cafe's cuisine, his continued application of

Scotch to every form of liquid on the table, and his sheer determination to make nice. He tried to draw me out on sports, but I had not seen a newspaper in months. Politics fell through for similar reasons, though we would certainly have argued if I had been up to date. But I was perversely proud of presenting an opaque surface to the usual concerns. On Johnson's initiative, we did venture briefly and self-consciously into Cézanne, of whose work Hannah's father and I both approved, though we were not able to get far in saying why this was so, as the conversation began creaking like strained pond ice at the first weight of any serious view. Mostly, I just drank.

Hannah sat and glowered through all our antics, silent for the most part but occasionally contributing a sarcasm. Every time I looked her way she rolled her eyes back in her head as if she were dying in that very instant.

And so dinner dragged by. We did not actually risk any talk of substance until dessert, at which point Hannah's father poured one last shot of the whiskey into his coffee, pushed away the crumbs of his apple pie, and sat back in his chair.

"So—" he said to Hannah. "I understand that you've decided to take some time off from school."

Hannah laughed. "I've dropped out, Daddy."

Johnson shrugged. "Whatever," he conceded, still amiably enough, but I saw the edge of the trial lawyer in him for the first time: *The prosecution is willing to stipulate* . . . "The point is, where do we go from here?"

"*We* don't go anywhere. You go back to New York. And Jeremiah and I go back to the studio and get on with our life."

I wished that she would stop calling me Jeremiah. But she

seemed to feel it added legitimacy to our case. I suggested, "You should be proud of your daughter, sir. She's a gifted musician."

"Oh, I know *that,*" Johnson snapped. "Don't think I'm unaware. Hell, *I* wanted her to go to Juilliard. I was prepared to pay—"

Hannah laughed derisively. "For me to spend my life playing scales and performing dead people's music."

"For you to properly learn your instrument," her father persisted. "You can go anywhere with a classical training. But no, you learn three chords and get somebody to leave a dollar in your hat at a coffeehouse and you think you can make a living playing any damn thing. You're young and you're pretty and you think the universe will hold you up. But it's not that simple, sweetheart, even if you've got the talent. Besides, at some point, you're going to want to have a family—"

Hannah rose abruptly. "I don't need this."

"Honey, I'm not trying to browbeat you. I'm just wondering if you've thought this thing through. The, uh, two of you."

He sincerely thought he was being supportive. But Hannah's dander was up. I'd seen her go after Burton often enough with that same look in her eye, so I was actually relieved when she just said, "I shouldn't have come tonight. I knew I shouldn't have come. I didn't mean to give you the impression that I'm open to persuasion." And she turned and walked out of the restaurant without looking back.

Hannah's father and I sat for a moment in silence. I looked at my empty water glass and realized that I was drunk and that it was going to take a real effort of concentration to get up onto my feet and walk out of there after Hannah with any dignity.

"I didn't really think I'd be able to change her mind," Johnson confided ruefully. "I just wanted to get a sense of the situation."

My heart went out to him, perhaps because I was drunk, perhaps just because I was young and condescending and believed his generation's bones would be ground beneath the plow of the glorious future our art would usher in. I said, "Little girls grow up."

"I've got a few connections in the art world in New York—gallery owners and such. I think I could even find a gig or two for Hannah in a couple clubs I know. And Juilliard's not the only music school in the City—"

I understood that we were being offered a deal of sorts—a plea bargain. Clearly our presumption was enormous, but if we pled guilty to the lesser charge of simple artistic ambition, he would do what he could to get us off with three-to-five in a competent art school and some showings in SoHo.

But I wanted the whole banana, the leap into the void, the thing so new it scorched the paint off the walls—I would rather have fried at that point than have accepted a success I could understand. I looked drunkenly at our four hands on the table, acutely conscious that I had some blue paint on my knuckle and some yellow under my fingernail. The nails of George Johnson's square competent hands were beautifully manicured, of course. But they weren't Hannah's hands.

"I think we'll just see where the path we're on is going, thanks," I told him and got up to leave. But George Johnson reached for my arm and held me for a moment, his grip surprisingly strong.

"If anything happens to her, I swear you'll have to answer to me," he declared in a low, fierce tone. "I'll be after you with a horsewhip, I swear to God I will."

"How remarkably old-fashioned," I said. I pulled my arm loose and wobbled out. Really, I had had way too much of that Scotch. George Johnson watched me go, his blue eyes cool and narrow, more calculating than angry. He had made his offer, after all, and made his threat: I got the sense he felt he had done what he could. Hannah's father was a decent, cunning, even dangerous man in his own way, but he was no match for his daughter.

When I got back to the barn studio Hannah was playing scales. I was astounded; she had made a great point in the past of scorning rote technique. But suddenly she was very fierce about it. Up and down, up and down the scale of C. Do re mi fa so la ti do. And again, from the top. She was obviously furious with me and didn't say a word for quite a while. I stood by the stove trying to keep one side of my body warm, looking for solid ground in a universe made sloshy with Scotch while the room swam around me.

At last Hannah stopped and looked at me. "So, did you boys get it all worked out? Got my future all set up?"

"I left him with the check," I told her defensively. Somehow it did not sound nearly so heroic and defiant in the saying as I had hoped it might when I began the sentence.

"You couldn't have *wrestled* the check from him," Hannah said disgustedly. "And you couldn't have paid it if you had. God, Mason, you sat there all night and drank his booze and smiled at his jokes and let him treat you like a son-in-law he was going to give the family business to."

"What was I supposed to do, tip over the table? Hannah, the poor guy loves you. Stupidly, sure, but—"

"And you love me too and that makes everything all right. We all can suffocate, I guess, if we call it love."

There seemed to me to be a lot of nightmare truth to this, but I was finding it difficult just then to continue the discussion and avoid throwing up at the same time. For some time, then, I avoided throwing up and left it at that. Hannah gave up on me after a while and went back to her scales. She must have played until three or four in the morning, long after I had staggered to the cold mattress and passed out, because my alcoholic dreams were all of staircases that just went on and on.

The next morning Hannah was back at the scales first thing. I awoke hung over and nursed my headache through a long morning to the vertiginous scale of C. She tried a couple of songs, cursing at every missed note, then went back to the absolute basic do re mi, again and again. Suddenly nothing she had ever played was good enough.

All through the morning and into the afternoon she played, and I watched her moving further and further away into a furious mechanicality poisoned with resentment. I tried a few of the tried-and-true endearments that had been our joy for months, but like the old songs, suddenly, all the words of our love sounded a little trite.

As if to mock my feeble efforts to reestablish rapport, George Johnson swept through one last time, just after noon. On his way out of town, he had decided to buy a painting. I believe it was a gesture of peacemaking on his part, but nothing could have injured me more in Hannah's eyes at that point than her father's patronage. Ignoring Hannah's stony glare and my dismay, he rummaged boldly through my works, found a large canvas showing Hannah playing her guitar on the stool by the window, and promptly offered me a thousand dollars for it.

"Forget it," I told him. "It's not for sale. If you want it, take it."

"Nonsense," Johnson said. He wrote the check, tore it out with a flourish, and set it on the table, then kissed his expressionless daughter good-bye and hauled the painting down the steps. The tires of his rented Oldsmobile spun on the frozen dirt road as he drove off, unnerving the cows.

Hannah and I looked at each other.

"The guy is a force of nature," I said.

"Isn't he, though," she replied coolly, and turned back to her scales.

I suppose that if I had never cashed that check the relationship might have been saved. But maybe not even then. I only knew how to do one thing well at that point in my life, and that was stand there in front of something with a canvas or a sketch pad and listen to the lines and colors. And somehow, in the obscure, fierce abyss of that, something would move and find its way into form. But Hannah needed more than that. She needed wisdom and perspective and kindness and real love that didn't suffocate or turn stale, and all of those things were in short supply during my long cold apprenticeship. And so in the end she went to California.

I have the impression in retrospect that it all happened instantly, but I know in fact that it took several unhappy weeks, because the last big snow that year came on the first weekend in May and that was the weekend Hannah left. She had already been talking for quite a while by then about getting out of the stifling atmosphere of Utah, where it was impossible to feel free enough to do real art. She had stopped doing her scales— just as her technique began to improve noticeably—and spent her days reading *The Making of a Counter Culture,* Herbert Marcuse, and Norman O. Brown. There was a spiritual revolution going on in California and she wanted to man the spiritual barricades. It seemed to me, though, that the spiritual barricades are wherever you find yourself in this world and that Hannah was running away.

"We've just got to stick it out," I told her.

She rolled her eyes disdainfully. "Right. Like barnacles."

I could find no immediate reply to this. Hannah's repartee invariably left me flailing. She had three brilliant thoughts to my vague one. My inarticulacy had charmed her, once upon a time—she'd filled in all my blanks with music. But now, I knew, she suspected I was a little stupid.

I couldn't blame her, really. It had been a grueling stretch of weeks, shot through with a kind of embarrassment at how lame all our posturings suddenly seemed. In the aftermath of her father's visit we had been snappy with each other and sunk back into ourselves. It was the sort of bad stretch that any marriage endures any number of times, but to Hannah and me such evidence of our irritable humanity seemed catastrophic. We were prepared only for radiance.

As my silence went on, Hannah shook her head in exasperation. "I don't see why you can't just come *with* me. We're in a rut—that's all. We've got to shake things up."

"I just don't see how running off to California is going to help anything."

"It's a leap of faith," she persisted.

"I thought *this* was a leap of faith."

"It was. But we need a new leap."

I considered the canvas of my work-in-progress—a rock landscape, as luck would have it, an unfocused dance of gray masses, barely begun and slow to develop, beneath a sky that needed work. Hannah's impatient leaps of faith, her impulsiveness, her lust for the flight into the Big Unknown, were what I loved most in her. But I knew that it was going to take me weeks, if not years, to get this landscape right, and I couldn't imagine a single thing in California that would help me do so.

Hannah waited for me to respond; then, taking my long, somewhat stubborn silence for response, she turned away. She already had a map of California, and she was tracing out her route in red.

I know now, looking back, that we had gotten to the emptiness, the place where you have used up what you know and what makes you feel secure. In other words, we had just gotten to the place where real art begins. But it is one thing to pledge your life to canvas or guitar—or another person—and something else entirely to wake up every morning as your same dumb self and face the naked day. Throw in the pressure of a feeble idealism that needs breakthroughs and revelations every fifteen minutes and there will almost inevitably come a point where you suspect that you should be seeking greener pastures.

Plus, let's face it, we were two kids who hadn't even begun to learn how to really love another human being, much less live with one. I see the moment go by again and again, like the brass ring beside a merry-go-round. Hannah is standing by the stove, warming her hands, or by the window, looking out; or she is sitting on the stool, tuning her guitar. The silence in the loft has been dead weight for days, since the last harsh words were said. I can see by the angle of her shoulders that she needs a word, a touch, a look, the simplest saving note of tenderness, to break the spell. But I stand furious by the easel, shut away from her need, telling myself that art needs all I have to give. It is a lie, from fear. And so the moments pass.

I walked Hannah to the bus station on a Wednesday afternoon, feeling gloomy and defeated, as the first deceptively gentle flakes began to fall. The trees had all been fooled into budding by a mild April; a lot of apple and apricot blossoms went down in that storm. The Greyhound stop in town was, appropriately enough, right in front of the American Hotel Cafe. We bought two cups of coffee to go and waited on the bench outside, letting snow accumulate on our shoulders. We sat in silence for a time—most of the arguing had been done by then. I knew Hannah believed she was leaving me to my mediocrity.

"Oh, cheer up, Mason," Hannah chided me at last, painfully jovial. "Look on the bright side—at least now you can go back to LeeAnne."

I said nothing, baffled as always by the swiftness of her assault on the partial truth. It was true enough that I had missed LeeAnne deeply, despite the debacle I had wrought with her. LeeAnne's golden contentedness, the way she made the daily round of life a thing of beauty, could never be anything but precious to me. But I never wanted Hannah to leave, as I had never wanted to leave LeeAnne. What I wanted, clearly, foolishly, was what the heart always wants, which is *everything.*

The bus appeared out of the gray-white haze at the east end of Main Street. Hannah stood up, a small pile of snow sliding off her coat. We had checked that morning's paper and noted that it was 72 degrees in Berkeley.

I stood up too, feeling like I was lifting a weight. The bus pulled up, its air brakes wheezing. The driver popped the tin door open and hustled down to check for baggage. But Hannah, the only passenger boarding that day, was traveling light—just her guitar and a single bag that would fit in the overhead rack. The driver punched her ticket, then moved on into the cafe to grab some coffee for the road. Hannah turned to me.

"There's still time for you to come," she said, a little cruelly, like someone teasing a dog on a short chain.

"To California?" I said. "I don't think so. But write me if you find gold."

Hannah smiled. Her confidence in her destiny was showing. Nothing bad could happen to her until she really learned how to play the guitar and she hadn't picked up her guitar for weeks. It had occurred to her that she might never learn to play it, in which case she would be immortal.

The driver reappeared, a skinny, nervous guy with a mammoth styrofoam cup of coffee.

"Off we go," he said briskly. "We gotta beat this storm out of here, all aboard now."

Hannah kissed me like a sister, abstracted, already on her way. A fierce, sharp despair rose in me; I knew that I had come up short. It was the first time in my life that I had felt that.

"I'll write," Hannah promised.

I nodded, mute and miserable, and off she went to the land of dreams. The bus heaved west and disappeared in the blurring white of the falling sky. She'd gotten out of town just in time, as it turned out—another half an hour and she'd have been snowed in with the rest of us for the next three days. Of course, in the long run, nothing would have kept Hannah Johnson in Utah.

I walked back to the barn studio, congratulating myself that I had stayed to face the emptiness while Hannah had fled for moonbeams. All through the last storm of that winter, I felt justified by the weather in my bleak and brittle peace, and painted apocalyptic voids. But as the icicles began to drip outside the windows and the ground began to show at last for good, it was harder—nothingness and springtime, as T. S. Eliot noted, are a brutal combination. I worked on my rocky landscape with a barnacle-like tenacity, clinging to the accumulating mass of painted stone until at last one day I looked at the overwrought canvas and found it hollow with a kind of avoidance.

Finally, about a month after Hannah left, I swallowed my pride and went to see LeeAnne. She had run through her pre-law boyfriend by then and was, astonishingly, prepared to be kind.

"Home is the sailor, home from the sea," she said, with just enough ironic bite to let me know she saw it clearly. I really had forgotten how deep her good nature ran.

## seven

# a walk in the blinding light

From wrong to wrong the exasperated spirit
Proceeds, unless restored by that refining fire
Where you must move in measure, like a dancer.

T. S. Eliot, "Little Gidding"

**Officer Lamar Barnes,** of the Nebraska Highway Patrol, had obviously not slept. He was probably a mournful-looking man even under the best of circumstances, but fatigue had darkened the natural bags under his eyes, partnering with gravity to accentuate the droopiness of his mild sad pink face. When the nurse ushered me over to him, he was sitting at a hospital desk, surrounded by paperwork and scrawled notes, a telephone prominent beside him. I could smell his tired sweat and sense his unhappiness the moment I came into the room. This good man had spent most of his night getting the bodies of Hannah and her companions out of their crumpled van; and he had spent the morning and afternoon calling their loved ones. By my estimation, his shift had run at least fourteen hours by that time and he wasn't finished telling people what they didn't want to hear.

He rose and extended his strong, square hand.

"Mr. Mason, thank you for getting here so quickly."

I shook his hand and sat down in the chair he indicated. Barnes sat back in his own chair, reaching automatically for a styrofoam cup of coffee. His Nordic blond hair was thinning and rumpled, and his shirt was tight at the belly with the first burgeoning of a cop's gut. The rest of his body was still lean, the arms browned precisely to the edge of his short-sleeved shirt.

"I know this can't be easy for you," he said reluctantly. "But obviously there are certain things we need to know, and certain things that need to be done."

"Of course."

Barnes turned back to his papers, seeking what comfort he could in procedure.

"As I said on the phone, I'm afraid I'm going to have to ask you to identify your friend. You are not required to do so, by any means. But obviously it would be a great help to us in, uh, sorting this out."

"I understand."

"All four of the people in the van were killed instantly. As far as we can tell, the deaths were impact deaths, not fire deaths. They didn't suffer. But I have to warn you—"

I was struck again by how harried and grieved Barnes looked. The night had stressed his features from early middle age into what he would look like ten years from now. I wondered what he was seeing in *my* face.

"I understand," I repeated.

"It isn't pretty." Barnes stood up. I stood up too. But still he hesitated.

"You knew Miss Johnson—is it *Miss* Johnson? She wasn't married?"

"Yes. I mean, no, Hannah wasn't married."

"You knew her well?"

"I loved her," I told him. "I don't know what the hell I knew."

We walked down a long corridor without speaking, then descended the most ordinary of echoing stairways to the basement. The door to the morgue stood unaccountably open to the hallway. Within, four bodies lay on separate gurneys, covered with heavy white sheets in a room with bare walls of concrete block painted a nightmare white.

"They don't get much traffic down here," Barnes noted apologetically, apparently referring to the open door and not the gurney occupants. But I was staring at those four draped forms and a sense of outrage was beginning to grow in me. That Hannah's dance with God should end in this bleak basement was unthinkable. Yet here she almost certainly was. It made me want to smash things.

Barnes led me into the room, which smelled sharply of some terrible industrial disinfectant. There was nothing much in there but the bodies and a small table by the wall. I had been prepared for layers of bureaucracy, forms and procedures, absurd wheels turning within wheels, but there wasn't even anyone else there. It seemed too obscenely simple, to just walk up to a gurney and lift the edge of a sheet.

At the first gurney, Barnes glanced at me and I nodded. He lifted the sheet and there was Hannah's body.

My stomach clutched; I retched and gagged. Barnes, that veteran, had a bucket ready and I puked into it gratefully. He stood looking slightly away, sympathetic and miserable, until I was done, then handed me a small white towel.

I wiped my mouth and looked back at her body. It was recognizable, but just barely. Wet wood burns slow, I always used to tell Hannah, denying her premonition of this day; but in the end Hannah had burned just fine.

Ah, you sweet, sad, beautiful girl, I thought. Why were you so sure about this?

"Mr. Mason—?"

"It's her."

Barnes reached for the sheet to cover her again, but I stopped him with a gesture. I bent and kissed Hannah's unburned forehead. It seemed almost to be something I owed her, to move through my horror and revulsion toward what I remembered of her; but all I felt was the skull through the thin cold flesh beneath my lips.

I straightened and replaced the sheet myself, carefully and gently. I took a step toward the door, but my legs didn't work and I fell onto the cold tile floor. I just lay there, stunned and strangely lucid, looking at the wheels on Hannah's gurney and tasting soot through the bile in my mouth.

In the end, it was Barnes who got me up off the morgue's floor and into a chair. He fetched me smelling salts and coffee, and stayed close with a hand on my elbow every time I moved. Before I left the basement I identified the rest of Hannah's bandmates as well, face by awful burned face, moving down the row of gurneys in a nightmare parody of efficiency, lifting each sheet in turn.

Upstairs again, the gentle normality of the hospital routine seemed unreal and flimsy. There was paperwork, at last—dispensations and authorizations. I knew exactly what I was supposed to do at this point because Hannah had been telling me what to do for twenty years: She had wanted to be cremated immediately, because she had been sure that if her family got hold of her body they would subject it to a Catholic funeral mass and bury it dolled up in some ridiculous dutiful daughter dress at ridiculous great expense. I even knew where I was supposed to take the ashes—to a wooded spot on the North Shore of Long Island not far from where Hannah had grown up, where she had used to sneak off as a teenager to play the kind of music her father despised. She swore that there was some kind of sparrow there that sang blues notes, which seemed unlikely to me. But I had directions to the place in a manila folder I had been carrying around for years, along with her handwritten will, the first draft of which had been written in the barn loft in Utah that first winter we lived together. The will had been a subject of much amusement to us then. I had gone through with the exercise mostly to humor her.

Now, revised and annotated at several points, the will had come into its own. There were three pages in the final version, with dates ranging from the seventies through the early nineties. Every stage had been witnessed by a notary public and Hannah's signature stood beside my own at the bottom of every page, with her initials and mine alongside every correction and amendment. Her father's daughter, she had taken great pride in the scrupulous legalities of it all, and she had believed the document to be unbreakable.

Barnes studied the pages unhappily. The earliest portions of the will had been written on the backs of pages torn from one of my Utah sketchbooks and had studies of cows and mountains and junipers and Hannah's own sweet face and hands on the other side. It did seem like a flimsy basis on which to authorize the incineration of a human body.

"You should at least call the family," he said, a little reproachfully.

"She was…alienated, I guess you could say, from her family. That's part of why she wanted it this way."

"You still should call them."

"I will," I promised. "I'll call them tonight. But that doesn't change what she wanted done."

"I suppose it doesn't." With obvious reluctance, he handed me the papers to sign that would authorize Hannah's cremation. There was only one funeral home in town and Barnes had no idea how long the procedure would take. He recommended that I stay overnight. We had a brief, surreal Chamber-of-Commerce sort of discussion of the various excellent and reasonably priced lodgings available near Golden, as if I had come for some fishing.

There was one last bit of business. In a room down the hall a table had been set up, its surface scattered with personal effects, including Hannah's acoustic guitar, miraculously undamaged, nestled in blue velvet within the hard eggshell of its sky-blue acrylic case. There was also a plastic-wrapped gift basket of Whole-Hearted Heartland Whole Wheat Bread and three flavors of jam, the kind of thing you can buy at any truck stop on I-80 between Laramie and Des Moines. The plastic had curdled around the edges from the heat, but otherwise the basket was still Suitable for Immediate Mailing and addressed, in Hannah's handwriting, to her father. There was someone's Saint Christopher medal, a scorched copy of *The Catcher in the Rye,* and a list of the other ruined contents of the van—amplifiers and drums, electric guitars and speakers, all the sad luggage of four people on a big trip cross-country in the grip of a dream.

Barnes had been standing unhappily to one side while I contemplated the table's contents. At last, perhaps to move me along, he cleared his throat.

"They were musicians?"

I nodded, grateful to be roused from my reverie. "The Blue Flame Band, on tour. Their first album just came out."

The policeman looked a little embarrassed, endearingly, to

not have heard of them. "I'm afraid I don't keep up with much of the newer sort of music. I suppose my daughter knows all about them."

"It's not like they were famous or something." To our further embarrassment, I began to cry.

The funny thing was, Hannah had not been the one who was driving the van. I knew by now that the driver had been Bedderman, the drummer, known to everyone as "Beat," an eminently sane soul with a perfect sense of rhythm who had fully intended to live until he was ninety. They had found him scorched in place, Barnes told me, still buckled into the driver's seat. They had to pry his hands off the wheel. The actual cause of the accident had apparently been a blowout of the left front tire.

It only made me feel worse to know this. It had been so much easier to be mad at Hannah, furious in the certainty that some fatal romantic gravity had turned the wheel in her hands. She had always loved that prophet's edge; careening glamorously toward martyrdom had suited her sense of truth. But not even Hannah could have made that tire blow, and certainly not from the passenger seat, where they had found her, still strapped in, seat belt firmly in place, her eyes wide open, gazing ahead. Not even death, so long and so patiently awaited, could make Hannah blink.

—

For a long time after Hannah went to California, I suspected that she had been just an incident in my life, an escapade, an aspect of my dreamy youth. While we had been together, I had believed with all my heart that our lives were wholly entwined; she had opened vistas of such beauty and richness to me that a single life did not suffice to sketch them. And then, in the course of events, I believed it had all been a siren's song. So many stories of seemingly fated things are told in hindsight by people willing to say they never doubted something for a moment, but this has not been the case in matters of my own soul. I lost faith a thousand times a day for years, and lose it now a thousand times a day. Even now I am certain only that everything I have of love in my life has come to me as grace, anew, from the ashes of my faithlessness, through the fire of my doubt.

So I did my best to write Hannah off. Circumstances conspired to make this easy. I opened a little show that spring in about six square feet of the university art gallery, but my series of ox-herding paintings, a year's work, failed to excite any interest. The single review in the local paper focused, as I had, on the muddiness of the postmodern American terrain, but less sympathetically; and the reviewer neglected, as I apparently had, to note the overarching spiritual context. Nothing moved anyone; certainly nothing sold. The paintings were taken down after three days to be replaced by a bumper crop of crayon Easter pictures from the local second-graders.

I got thrown out of my barn studio a few weeks later when the farmer who owned the place found several nude studies of Hannah. By then the eviction seemed appropriate, a delayed punishment for relentless sins of unreality. I moved in with LeeAnne, a real house of our own, with real rent, on Eighth North Street in town. There were actual utilities, lights, heat, and running water, and of course utility bills. Obviously it was time to buckle down and be a grownup, and I found a part-time job as a housepainter. It seemed like the only way I could earn honest money applying color to surfaces.

LeeAnne encouraged me in every aspect of my feeble realism, as patient with me as a mother teaching a child to walk. She felt briskly pragmatic herself at this point. She had entered a decidedly Freudian phase and was bent on forsaking the misery of neurosis for the unhappiness of the actual world. She was writing down all her dreams, and encouraged me to do so as well, but my dreams were still too much of Hannah then and I didn't want to analyze them, frankly.

LeeAnne's dreams sufficed for both of us, though. She was a lush, sensuous dreamer and recalled every detail. Often we would lie in bed for an hour or more after waking, and even longer on weekends, while she retraced her labyrinthine dream steps with me. Her dreams were full of flowers and flight and wise old women and good sex with interesting people. Often the good sex with interesting people occurred in other times and places, in ancient Judea or Salem, Massachusetts, and usually at great personal risk. (LeeAnne was having what she would later come to think of as past-life dreams but she attributed them to a costume-drama history phase she'd gone through in the fourth grade.) I would lie enwrapped with her and listen contentedly, breathing in her sweet blond air.

I painted in the mornings and housepainted in the afternoons, while LeeAnne pursued the final courses for her degree in psychology *magna cum laude* and plotted her assault on graduate school. She was a sort of phenomenon in her department—a burst of fresh air, bright, funny, innocent, commonsensical, and enthusiastic all at once. All the professors had crushes on her. They wanted her to be a professor too, but LeeAnne wanted to Heal. In her own mind, she had majored in Healing.

As the months passed and our reunion lost its tentative, convalescent quality, LeeAnne and I began to relax into a quiet, deepened joy in our life together. Some evenings we would walk up the hill hand-in-hand to watch the dollar movies at the university theater or hear the Utah Symphony, up from Salt Lake to spread culture in the provinces: LeeAnne's student card worked wonders everywhere. Most nights we stayed at home and read good books, or played little card games and listened to the Jazz Hour on the radio, basking in a sweet, familiar ceremoniality we were just beginning to trust again. It was in many ways an idyllic time, though every once in a while a letter from Hannah would show up.

These were not good days. I would come in from work with the atrocious lime or canary yellow of somebody's new dining room ceiling all over me and the letter would be lying on its own table, quarantined from the rest of the mail. LeeAnne would be in the other room doing something energetically. A lot of our minor household cleaning got done on those days when a letter from Hannah came—I always read the latest from Berkeley to a background chorus of abrasives applied, and deep scrubbing, continued scrubbing, sad, pained, furious scrubbing. Our porcelain and countertops gleamed with the difficulty of it all.

Hannah herself was vigorous, enthusiastic, and neglecting

her guitar. I keenly felt the impact of California's spiritual tourist culture in those early letters from Berkeley. Hannah was meditating and eating vegetarian and marching on the weapons lab at Livermore, much as a new arrival in Paris would see the Louvre and the Eiffel Tower and walk a lot in the Luxembourg Gardens and along the Seine. She had had her astrology chart done. She could feel her chakras opening. She had three lovers, one of them a woman. And always, always, as she wrote in her letters, she loved me with a love that was broad and free. By implication, my love for her was earthbound and constrained, which was true enough. I suspected Hannah was fooling herself and pissing away her talent.

Not that I wasn't. This was a period of dispirited imitations and parody in my own work, full of faux Cézannes and knock-offs of early Kandinsky. I was using color again half-heartedly, after the collapse of my muddy ox-herding palette, and seeing with a cynical eye, caught halfway between landscape and abstraction. But at least I was failing at *art,* as I saw it, in the good old traditional way. I would drink myself to death or go nuts or kill myself in due time, but meanwhile I was failing miserably right where I was supposed to be failing, in the studio and in my domestic life, while Hannah had fled the work on dry land for a cruise package of phony bliss.

When I had finished the letter I would fold it up and put it in my back pocket and go find LeeAnne in the kitchen or the bathroom or wherever she was scrubbing away. She would not look up as I came into the room. She just kept scrubbing, her

jaw set, her back bent, all her weight going into some irre-
movable stain.

"How's Hannah?" she would always ask, resignedly. And I
would answer, resignedly, "She's doing some damned California thing."

"Good for her," LeeAnne would say. And she would scrub
and scrub and scrub, while I stood there uselessly, until at last I
would go and begin to make dinner. I always made dinner on
the days a letter from Hannah came, and I always did the dishes
afterward, in the clean fresh sink. Often, with luck and delicacy,
LeeAnne and I would even be okay again by then, and we
would play some cards or listen to the Jazz Hour on the radio.

One night, almost exactly a year after Hannah went to California, I dreamed that I had followed her footsteps through a
blizzard, and then, as night fell, through freezing darkness,
making my way in the storm on my hands and knees, finding
where Hannah had stepped by touch, by a desperate Braille of
temperature difference, by the minutely warmer quality of the
ice and snow where her feet had passed, or by some memory
of music on the whirling frozen air, and then finding where
she had been simply by pain and the deepening ache of emptiness, as if suffering itself were a sense like a bloodhound's sense
of smell.

At last the trail led to a broken place in the mountain's
heart, into the cleft and womb of a cave, and I lost her completely in the mute and scentless rock. At the center of the cave

a fire burned, without heat, with a warmth that warmed the eyes only, and it seemed to me that Hannah must have gone there, right into the heart of the lucid flame. There was nowhere else she could have gone. But I could not follow.

In the dream, I lay for a long time on the cold stone floor, frozen and exhausted and disheartened, only gradually becoming aware in the fire's subtle light that the walls of the cave were covered with ancient paintings, that the stone was alive with dancing deer and cosmic graffiti, the vibrant images of forty thousand years. There was an empty spot on the wall, a stretch of naked stone like the tissue of a scar, and I began to paint there myself, finding color as I had found Hannah's footsteps in the snow. As I painted, it seemed to me that I had been in that cave for forty thousand years myself and knew every image there by heart, that I had found each of them on that rock as I was finding the image before me now, by an ache.

I painted through the dream's night, through every layer of loss and the strange impersonal remembrance of the images, until the fire began to warm me at last and I painted as the fire burned down, unhurried at last and at peace, and as daylight began to show outside, I found that I was in some sort of chapel and that it was my wedding day. I was wearing my housepainter's overalls and the panel of the mural I had been working on was finished. Outside, LeeAnne waited, radiant in a white dress, looking as free and beautiful as I had ever seen her, maybe even freer and more beautiful, as if something in my eyes had burned away through that long night with the rest of the fire's stubborn fuel and I could see her for once as she really was.

When I woke the next morning the room was filled with spring sunlight and the air was warm and soft. I lay still, savoring the peace, listening to the birds until LeeAnne woke up. Then I kissed her drowsy eyelids and told her about the dream, sparing no detail. She was pleased that I had dreamed up such a pleasant wholesome scene and launched immediately into various interpretations. It could mean something Oedipal, obvious womb symbolism, and so forth.

"No," I said. "I think it means that we should get married."

LeeAnne blinked, and smiled. "Really?"

We were married two weeks later in the quietest of civil ceremonies downtown, on a glorious afternoon in late May, avoiding the complex of weighty expectations inherent in a June wedding. The weather that year had been kind and all the fruit had set on the trees already. The only snow in sight on that balmy day was on the peaks across the valley. LeeAnne wore a short-sleeved dress of sleek white satin and a red hibiscus blossom in her hair. I wore the only decent shirt I had and a pair of dark slacks without a drop of paint on them. Her parents came up from Cedar City, and mine from Virginia, but otherwise we kept the ceremony simple and small. A few of LeeAnne's friends from the Psychology Department threw rice. Burton, in whiteface, was the best man, and the bridesmaid, one of LeeAnne's old roommates, who had never really liked me, came down with the flu at the last moment. Afterward LeeAnne and I walked home contentedly hand-in-hand and put her bouquet in a vase of water, because there had been no one there to toss it to but Burton, who had mimed an extravagant effort to catch it and let it drop.

I had written Hannah a somewhat cautious letter informing her of the wedding, striving to sound neither apologetic nor defensive. We had after all vowed to stay in touch, and to remain friends; Hannah had been insisting for a year now that she was grateful we were no longer constrained by romance. The baby steps our nascent friendship had been taking by mail, however, did not seem to me to have prepared us for so challenging a dance. I had no idea whether Hannah would laugh and say "I told you so," or weep, or hate my guts.

About a week after the wedding, though, Hannah sent us an audio tape with half a dozen of her latest compositions—songs intended, I believe, to convey her blessing on the marriage. It was like her to believe in the pure transmission of music from heart to heart without complication, but none of us was really up to such high standards then. LeeAnne just set the package aside in our customary postal quarantine; she never did listen to that particular mix of songs. But I remember one of them very well and it wasn't a wedding song at all. It was called "Hell and Back (A Walk in the Blinding Light)," and though Hannah had claimed in her brief cover letter that she was wholly without bitterness, I have to say that I wasn't so sure myself. The song went, in part:

> *I've done the crucifixion, babe—*
> *I've done the little hell—*

*I've done the nights in the lonely tomb*
*in the house that we knew too well.*

*And I could have stayed*
*and we could have prayed*
*and built dams against the loss*
*but in the end there's still the river*
*and in the end there's still the cross*

*and forty days of walking around*
*like a whisper out of the night,*
*like a song you forgot, or you never quite knew,*
*like a walk in the blinding light.*

I came back out to the waiting area in the Golden hospital carrying Hannah's guitar in its monogrammed blue case, and the ridiculous basket of bread and jam she had intended to send to her father. By the clock, what had seemed to me an endless loop through hell had taken not quite half an hour. Sammy was still sitting where I had left him and he looked up at me with that same bright terrible innocent hope I had left him with. I took him in my arms, and we wept.

The sky had clouded over, as promised, by the time we came out of the hospital. On the western horizon lightning flashed in the heart of a black sky. As we got into the car and drove in silence to the motel Barnes had recommended, fat raindrops began to slap against the windshield. Sammy had left the air conditioner on in his earlier fiddlings with the controls.

I reached to turn it off, but managed to turn the radio on instead. And there, on good old KHRZ, the "Heart of Rock and Roll in the Heartland," was the Blue Flame Band singing "Hell and Back (A Walk in the Blinding Light)," the breakout single from their first album.

I moved to turn it off, but Sammy stopped me.

"It's Hannah," he said reproachfully.

And I let it be, because, of course, it was. We drove on into the thunderstorm, listening and pained, alone with the music and our hearts. In the smeared windshield, I could see Hannah's ruined body before me, wiped away by every beat of the windshield wipers and returning in the next wave of rain, while the Blue Flames played that good old country blues.

*And you still don't get it, even now,*
*though I'm saying it plain and true:*
*I've been through the pain and the dark and the flame*
*and what's left is my love for you.*

*And it's almost sunrise now, babe*
*and there's no grief left in sight*
*and I'm tipping that boulder over*
*for a walk in the blinding light.*

# h e l l - b e n t

Only Love, only Love, only Love—
how many times must I repeat it
before you leap into the fire?

Rumi

—

*In the motel room,* while Sammy took a bath, I gave LeeAnne a call. The phone on her separate line at home rang four times before her answering machine kicked in, her bright professional voice, full of compassion and millennial wisdom: "Hi, this is LeeAnne Mason, I'm okay, you're okay, and the ways of God are a gentle ever-deepening mystery, so even though we missed each other it will all work out over the course of many lifetimes and if you're calling about this week-end's seminar call 767-2676 and ask for Janet."

All this with Central African hunter-gatherers chanting in the background to a synthesizer beat. I normally avoided the karmic loop of LeeAnne's answering machine. But I was so hungry for the sound of her voice that I stayed on the line through it all this time in the hope that she was just screening her calls.

"Hi," I said after the beep. "This is your husband from the present lifetime calling. It's the twentieth century, getting along toward the end, and I just wanted to—"

There was a rustle at the other end, and then LeeAnne's real voice, slightly breathless. "Jerry?"

"Hi sweetie."

We both paused, suffering a series of phone noises, squawks and beeps and whirrings, as the machine begrudged us the interruption. When the process was finished at last, LeeAnne said, "Sorry about that."

"A small price to pay for human contact."

"God, I'm so glad you called. Are you okay? Where are you?"

"In the Golden Inn. It looks like we're going to have to stay over for a night or even two."

"Is there a problem?"

I hesitated, baffled as always by LeeAnne's deep, instinctive pragmatism, wondering what could possibly constitute a problem at this point. Was it a problem that Hannah was dead? I could not feel it to be so—the scale was blown. There were no problems. I simply felt in my heart that the best part of me had disappeared into a tangle of metal and a ball of flame and that what lived on was going through the motions in a nightmare. And Hannah's wrecked form floated before my mind's eye even now, imperturbably, horribly, whether I blinked or not. No, there was no problem.

LeeAnne seemed to sense that it was not the moment to sweat over the fine points. "How's Sammy?"

"He's okay, as far as I can tell. You know Sammy."

"I do. That's why I'm so worried."

"He cried a bunch at the airport in Houston."

"That's a good sign," averred LeeAnne, who fervently believed this. Her past-life clients dipped regularly into the catastrophes of history and wept cleansing rivers; catharsis ruled and redeemed, in the world according to LeeAnne.

I realized that I was beginning to get testy. In the bathroom, Sammy's splashing in the tub had ceased. No doubt he was listening intently, alive to every incomprehensible nuance while his parents negotiated the big issues. I said, "I suppose it is."

She picked up on my tone at once. We were silent for a moment, one of those long chess-game-in-progress pauses at the crucial points in the conversations of the long-married, each of us going over the various move sequences open to us. We both were grandmasters in our small game and knew what every move and word implied.

LeeAnne decided first: no fight tonight. "Have you talked to her father yet?"

"I'm calling him next," I told her, grateful for the change of tack.

"God, Jerry."

"I know. God knows how he'll take it. He once threatened to horsewhip me if anything ever happened to his little girl."

"Oh, he can't possibly blame *you* for this," LeeAnne

exclaimed instantly, offended by the very idea. "His little girl was hell-bent."

"I suppose she was," I conceded, feeling the sweet, sad truth of that for a moment, a clean little flare of the real grief through all the smoke and fuss of my punier issues and confusions. "Hell-bent" had always been LeeAnne's slightly fastidious way of saying what I had loved most in Hannah.

LeeAnne heard this too, of course; and we were silent again. Because it was my grief itself that grieved LeeAnne most.

In the other room, Sammy stirred in his cooling bathwater.

"Did you want to talk to the kid?"

"Of course."

I began to gather up the phone's cord, which looked like it had a good chance of reaching to the tub.

"So how long do you think all this is going to take?" LeeAnne asked, as I started toward the bathroom.

"I'm not exactly sure. I'll know more tomorrow."

"Are you all *right,* Jerry? I mean, how are you actually *doing* with all this?"

"I'm fine," I told her, which was so patently ridiculous that we both just let it go. At the door of the bathroom, I held up the phone. "Sam, do you want to talk to your mother?"

He looked dubious. "Will I get electrocuted?"

I blinked. "What?"

"If I talk to her from the tub," he persisted. "With the water and all—will I get electrocuted?"

"No," I said firmly. "No way, man, I wouldn't let that happen to you. A phone doesn't have that kind of electricity running through it."

"He doesn't want to talk to me?" LeeAnne said in my ear, her voice suddenly small and hurt.

"No, no," I reassured her. "It's nothing like that. He's just worried about the phone and the bathwater. He's in the tub."

"Because if he doesn't want to—"

"LeeAnne, sweetheart. It's okay. Really. It's just technical difficulties." I handed the phone to Sammy, who persisted in treating it like a live wire. Which hurt me too, of course: so obvious did it seem to me that his confidence in my judgment had been damaged. I hadn't been able to protect Hannah and I wasn't going to be able to protect him. Clearly none of us was getting through this with our sense of certainty intact.

But Sam relaxed at the sound of LeeAnne's voice. I ran a little more hot water into the tub so he didn't get cold, then left the two of them to their conversation. From the other room, I could hear the ease and relief in Sammy's voice as he chattered away to LeeAnne about the airplane ride and what our rental car looked like. LeeAnne even had him laughing soon. He could cry with her and he could laugh with her and he was going to spend the rest of his life, I was quite sure, recovering from her insecurity, and from the shame and guilt and gloom he absorbed on a regular basis from me, and from the loss of Hannah. Just another American family, hell-bent.

—

We had been married for about a year, a round of the vivid Utah seasons, when LeeAnne decided it was time to have a baby. She figured that if we timed it right we could fit it in between her master's and her Ph.D. On a roll professionally and personally, she felt that she was getting in touch with her real needs at last, and one of those needs was a baby. The other was a house, but she felt that she could wait a bit on the house. The baby, on the other hand, had some urgency to it. Once she started working on her Ph.D., LeeAnne calculated, it would be at least five years before another "window" opened.

It made sense to me. By now I had passed beyond weak parodies of the modern masters into utterly feeble abstractions of my own and was wholly at sea. My palette was watery and all my forms leaked. I was lost, in my art and in my life, with no land in sight and no real sense of imminent landfall, and so I agreed with LeeAnne that some real-world responsibility was probably just what I needed. LeeAnne was increasingly concerned with the drifting and diffuse nature of my vocation, and not just for the sake of my soul. At parties now with her fellow grad students and professors, all of them on well-defined tracks, she found herself somewhat embarrassed and at a loss when they asked, as they inevitably did, what her husband *did*.

"Tell them I'm a housepainter," I told her.

"I can't tell them that. It's flippant. They're talking about your *career.*"

"Then tell them I'm a drunk."

LeeAnne just rolled her eyes. She tried for a while to tell them boldly and proudly that I was an artist, but that felt too weak. She didn't believe it herself at that point, I suppose, though she had found it charming enough during her undergraduate days. In any case, she couldn't say, when pressed, what it *was* that I painted anymore (aside from living room walls, I mean); I had stopped doing those nice landscapes and the realistic sketches that everyone liked so much. So naturally enough, in the face of my obscurities, LeeAnne began to tell people that we were going to have a baby. At least in that regard it was obvious what I did.

LeeAnne's doctor told her she should hold off on conceiving for a couple months after she stopped taking the Pill, to let her system get back to a condition in which motherhood seemed chemically attractive to it again. Throughout that November and December she and I practiced the archaic chastity of those for whom pregnancy is the consequence of sexual intercourse. We were as tender with each other as if we were going into battle; all our small daily activities took on the poignancy that came with awareness of an imminent disruption. Her hand in mine on the walk to a movie could bring sudden tears to my eyes and one night the way she put fresh butter in the glass butter dish we had bought at a junk shop actually made me weep. It was as if my own hormones had gone wild in sympathy with LeeAnne's, as if my body and emotions were gathering themselves like hers for the coming adventure. We had invited the transforming angel in, and we both knew our lives were never going to be the same again.

As the new year approached, my usual insomnia sharpened until it seemed to me I lay awake all night beside a whetted sword. I would wait for the first sign of gray in the sky over the eastern mountains, then slip from the bed. While LeeAnne slept on, I would dress and go out to walk the quiet lanes of the town, up the hill and then across the campus and away, following the canal out of town toward the canyon's mouth. By the time it was light enough to see color I would be alone beyond the last of the houses, with the sheer gray mountains steep and close and the sun still held beyond them so that all the light was luminous and cool. I would slow, and then stop, letting all the peace in the dawn light settle into me, until the very trees around me, pines and junipers, came into focus as presences in a luminous hush, and whatever tree was closest to me showed itself as perfect, so that my gaze could rest on its simplest needle and find all of beauty there. I would stand poised in that clear hush, relieved of haste and need, sustained in the sight of that single pine while the slow light grew and my fear and pain and confusion settled away like silt from still water. Then all things seemed possible and there was nothing left to do but love, and see, and stand in the growing light while the sunrise showed first on the mountains across the valley to the west, a rose-colored breath on the peaks that crept downward like rosy dew toward the shadowed green valley floor.

When the sun slipped over the ridge above me at last and tore the sky into brightness, I would stir at the first warm touch as if stirring in a dream without awakening. Still held in the lingering luminosity, treating my condition like spun glass, like a bird in my hand or a fertile egg, I would start toward home with that lucidity cupped and sheltered within me, praying for it to last.

Some days I would even make it home without my mind resuming the usual compulsions. I would slip into the still-sleeping house and pause at the bedroom door while LeeAnne breathed slow and steady and beautiful in our bed. But I knew my mind and its clumsiness; and I knew that LeeAnne woke slowly: One kiss and an awkward word and we'd both be awake in the daily wakefulness that was a kind of dream itself. And so I let her sleep and headed for my studio, where it always seemed possible that the next empty canvas would ripen into something that would hint, at least, at those pine needles. And when LeeAnne woke later and shuffled to the doorway with her hair awry and her flannel nightgown trailing, I would kiss her good morning and say *yes, the walk was lovely, and pancakes would be great, and I love you more than the sunrise, sweetheart, more than rosy dawn itself.* This always made her smile.

At last January came. LeeAnne and I made tender, awestruck love night after night, and on certain perfect winter afternoons, and in the morning, almost every morning, offering all our energies to the promise of conception. We felt sober and consecrated and quietly jubilant and we ate exceptionally well, a diet high in proteins and complex carbohydrates to sustain all that consecrated sex. I even stopped drinking, which seemed to me to indicate that I was serious indeed. But one day toward the end of the month I came back from one of my early-morning walks to find LeeAnne emerging from the bathroom with a downcast air.

"What is it?" I said, alarmed.

She shrugged, indicating a stiff upper lip. "A little disappointment, is all. I got my period."

My heart surged with relief—the wrong relief, I recognized at once. I was delighted, monstrously and spontaneously, as though it were a reprieve. I knew in that instant that I had been lying to myself. But in the next beat, like thunder on the heels of lightning, I felt an enormity of dismay. Because it seemed to me, in the awful clarity of that flash, that our path toward happily ever after—the destiny we had believed to be whole and unified—had splayed like the needles of a pine.

LeeAnne had seen it instantly; she knew my face too well.

"You're not going to hold it against me, are you?" I asked, frankly pleading, not even attempting to dissemble, because in that moment there was nothing possible but the truth.

"I could never hold it against you," LeeAnne replied, with equal frankness. "But I think I'm always going to hate you for it."

That seemed fair enough to me. I held my tongue and fled to my studio, which was not a real studio at all but simply what should have been our living room and what would have been the baby's room, if there had been a baby.

LeeAnne and I lived with a terrible silence between us for

a month, as if some precious thing had been dropped beyond reach and there was nothing for that month but the horror of watching it fall. There never was a crash, there was just that terrible silence and what seemed at last like an endless fall into nowhere, into the gap where our future had been, until at last LeeAnne and I agreed that it might be best if I went away. She was in touch with her needs, after all; and now it seemed that I was in touch with mine; and in human psychology as we understood it then, that was that.

Burton gave me a ride out of town. He had intended to take me all the way to the bus station in Salt Lake City, but I had him stop at the top of the grade at the west end of the valley. I told him I would just hitchhike from there.

"You may not be able to get a ride here for a while," Burton noted, trying to dissuade me. "It's sort of the middle of nowhere."

I shrugged. The middle of nowhere sounded about right to me. We embraced and promised to write, and he got back in his car and drove back down into the valley.

I stood there for a long time at the point where the road disappeared into the mountains, beneath a snowy slope of aspens long past their golden autumn prime, with my cheap orange backpack on the ground beside me, filled with art supplies. It was still and quiet except for the cold February wind. Fifteen feet away from me a tough old pine tree held its ground. I tried half-heartedly to do my little mystic trick with the mountain quiet and that tree, but sometimes stillness is simply empty and sometimes a tree is just a tree.

Burton had been right, of course: There was almost no one going my way. It was almost an hour before someone finally stopped, a young guy in a green Rambler station wagon who asked me cheerfully where I was headed.

I hesitated over that, if only *pro forma*—I had told LeeAnne, and Burton too, that I had no idea where I was going. But I suppose I knew even then that I would end up in California. I had checked that morning's paper and in Berkeley it was 72 degrees.

After Sammy got off the phone with LeeAnne, I took a deep breath and tried to reach George Johnson, first at his office and then at home. But both calls reached only answering machines, a dispiriting double dose of Hannah's father's bluff recorded heartiness. I hesitated before committing myself to the second tape: "Hello, Mr. Johnson, this is Jeremiah Mason—" and then stopped, frozen, unwilling to simply deliver the blatant news to a machine and unable to find a single word to say otherwise. At last I just left him the phone number at the motel and hung up.

I put my face in my hands, ashamed and distraught, feeling like a bungling angel of death. When I looked up some time later, Sammy, wrapped in a towel, was peering at me from across the room. God knows how long he had been standing there.

"Are you all right, Dad?"

"I'm fine," I told him, rising with a guilty start. "Come on, let's get you dried off, you're dripping all over the rug."

"No. I can do it myself." Sammy retreated into the bathroom, closing the door behind him quietly but firmly, a soft click of reproach.

## nine

## the alpha and the omega

The sacrifices of God are a broken spirit:
a broken and a contrite heart, O God,
thou wilt not despise.

Psalm 51:17

---

*The rain had passed* by dinnertime. Sammy and I went out to walk the muggy streets of Golden. To the west, the sun was approaching the even, endless horizon, setting the lingering cumulus clouds aflame with rose and gold. A sunset chorus of sparrows animated Golden's embattled trees and the gutters gurgled cheerfully with runoff. On square lawns in front of the solid little houses, men raked up storm debris with a measured easy air, nodding as Sam and I passed by. On other porches, couples rocked and whiled away the cocktail hour with lemonade and iced tea. The driveways were filled with well-kept Buicks and Chevy pickup trucks and the sidewalks were peppered with bikes and dogs. It was a mid-American idyll of sorts, and one thought wouldn't go away: Hannah had found a lovely place to die.

On the main drag, we had dinner in a homey little diner, the waitress's banter with Sammy making everything easy and vaguely sad. It was precious normality and ease itself that were hurting me now, I realized; all the things that Hannah had surrendered so willingly and had seemed to render empty by her surrender. If everything was sacrifice, if all of life and life itself turned to smoke, then what did the burnt offering serve? Hannah had believed it was what God required of her, I knew. But I had to wonder, watching Sammy rise politely to the waitress's mothering and then sink back into his brooding as she walked away, whether God required too much.

The phone was ringing as we let ourselves back into the motel room. Sammy ran ahead and snatched the receiver up, obviously thinking it was LeeAnne. But his open face closed at once, as if he'd gotten lima beans when he'd expected ice cream. I was struck afresh, from across the room, by how much he could look like Hannah when the world did not go as he wished.

"Oh, hi Grandpa," he said.

I hurried over beside him to get the phone away, but Sammy was absorbed in his civility, in the awe of a long-distance call and the consciousness of crisis, and would not yield. Hannah, despite her own difficult relations with her father, had always made a great point of having Sammy spend time with him, and the two were on easy terms. I could hear the untroubled boom of George Johnson in the earpiece, asking him something about his most recent birthday present, a baseball glove. (Johnson and I unwillingly shared a quixotic vision of Sammy's future in professional sports.) Sammy told him the glove was great. His manner with his grandfather was grave and gracious and ever so slightly indulgent. His mother's son in this more than most things, he treated Johnson the way you might treat an overenthusiastic dog.

I gestured for Sammy to give me the phone. He nodded, but made no move to do so. "Uh-huh," he murmured to Johnson, his delicate Hannah-brows knitted in concentration. "Uh-huh."

*"Sammy—"* I insisted, sotto voce.

He covered the mouthpiece with his hand, which barely did the job. While George Johnson went on audibly in the receiver about the two of them catching a Yankees' game next time he was on the East Coast, Sammy confided to me, in a desperate whisper, "I don't know how to *tell* him, Dad."

My heart almost broke at that: the weight of the world on his little shoulders. I said, gently, "I'll tell him, Sammy."

He surrendered the receiver reluctantly.

"Hello? Mr. Johnson?"

"Jeremiah! Well now, hey there! Long time no see!"

It had been almost ten years, in fact, and by profound mutual agreement we had been content with the prospect of never seeing each other again. But I understood the cultural value of Johnson's heartiness—as with wolves, broad posturing from a distance is generally better than growls and the showing of teeth when you get too close.

"I'm afraid I'm calling with bad news, sir."

He dropped his big bluff tone at once. "Is it Hannah?"

"It is, sir. There was an accident, with the band's van. Hannah—"

"How bad?" he interrupted, peremptory, as if I were a hostile witness—knowing already, I think, but needing to try for that last handhold of control.

"She's dead, Mr. Johnson. I'm so terribly sorry. She was killed instantly. All four of them were."

The phone line hummed in my ear, an awful silence that went on and on.

"They're sure?" Johnson asked at last. "There's no possibility of a mistake?"

The image of Hannah on the gurney came to me again. I had trained my inner eye for decades, learning to hold an image steady. There was no way not to see her ruined body now; it was the central fact. It was simply what I saw, when I looked inside.

"There's no mistake. I'm so sorry, sir."

Another silence. I could almost hear his mind in it, circling the brute news sluggishly, staggered but still hoping for a reprieve.

And then a terrible sound came through the wire, not quite a gurgle, not quite a cry: a weird half-animal keening. It went on for almost ten seconds like the air bleeding out of a ruptured tire.

Another silence followed. When Johnson spoke at last, his voice was resigned, dignified, and even slightly, characteristically, aggressive. "When did it happen?"

"This morning, about three A.M. Nebraska time."

"Why didn't somebody call me right away?"

Hannah, I knew, would have given him the straight answer: *If your daughter had had her way, sir, they might not have called you at all.* But I said, "They weren't sure about the identification until about an hour ago."

"I see."

We were silent a moment. Across the room, Sammy was hunched furiously over his keyboard, playing something sporadic in a minor key. He'd set the volume low but in the silence the mournful notes stood out. Hannah's father exclaimed, "What the hell is that?"

"Sammy's working on a song."

"Ahh," he said, his voice softening; and then, "How's he taking this?"

"Hard," I allowed, as you would say Alaska is large. But Johnson seemed satisfied with the shorthand.

"He's a good boy. I see a lot of Hannah in him."

I made no reply, perhaps ungenerously.

Johnson took a breath. "So, what's next? Getting her home, I suppose. Arranging the funeral. God, I'm glad her mother didn't live to see this. Is that an awful thing to say? But I don't think any parent wants to outlive his child."

"No...Mr. Johnson, this is very difficult, but about the funeral—"

"I can wire you money, of course, for the, uh, transportation costs—"

"No, it's not that. It's—well, I have to be frank, sir. Hannah's will was very specific as to what she wanted done, at this point."

"Um-hm," Johnson said carefully, noncommittally.

"She wanted to be cremated immediately. And she wanted no memorial service, no funeral. Just a private scattering of the ashes at a spot on Long Island."

"Nonsense," Johnson snapped. "I mean, that's all very well, a lovely bohemian fantasy. But I could never allow my daughter's death to be treated as some casual existential gesture—"

"I don't think she conceived of the gesture as casual, Mr. Johnson. It was very important to Hannah."

"I can't believe we're arguing about this."

"It's no pleasure for me either, I assure you."

Johnson was silent a moment. "There's a will, you say?"

"Yes."

"Is it notarized?"

"Yes."

"Witnessed, signed, dated?"

"Yes," I said, marveling, realizing why Hannah had been so obsessive about the legalities of her will. Just because you're paranoid doesn't mean they're not out to get you.

"Have the authorities in Nebraska indicated they are prepared to honor the document?"

"Yes," I said wearily. "Look, Mr. Johnson—"

"Then I suppose I'll have to break it."

I paused. "What?"

"The will. Whatever damned hippie piece of paper you're basing all this nonsense on. I can break it."

His voice had a slight exultant note; the prospect of a legal battle had displaced his grief for the moment. My own duty here was clear enough, though I mentally cursed Hannah for imposing it. It was bad enough that she was gone; that I should now have to fight with her father over the disposal of her remains seemed degrading beyond words. But I had promised her, repeatedly, that I would go through with this absurd and ugly brawl.

"You can try," I told Hannah's father; and on that note we hung up.

Later that evening Sammy and I played cards to pass the time. We started out with Go Fish, but moved on, when he dismissed that as "for little kids," to a surprisingly complex kind of rummy that LeeAnne had taught him. I was preoccupied and glad just to be doing something harmless, but Sammy was intent on the unfolding game. He was at that stage of wanting very much to win but not yet being very good. I played as poorly as I could, but still failed to lose as many hands as his pride required. At last, he exclaimed in frustration that he would *never* be any good.

"Someday, you'll be *very* good," I told him, though I didn't add that by then the game would probably mean nothing to him.

I hitchhiked into Berkeley on a balmy day in early February of 1982 to find all the cherry trees in spectacular pink bloom. I would have preferred more miserable weather, to fit my mood—I had been perfectly content nearly freezing to death in the Sierras—but the premature spring did reinforce my suspicion that I had journeyed to a land of lotus-eaters. In my heart it was winter still.

My last ride dropped me off at the corner of Bancroft and Telegraph Avenue. In my pocket were thirty-five dollars, a nub of charcoal pencil, and Hannah's address. I walked the two blocks past the pizza shops and record stores, through a crowd of beggars and students and general free spirits, through the secondhand smoke and competing music and a buzzing host of sidewalk tables selling crystals and tie-dyed T-shirts, palm readings and pendants. I kept thinking *No, Toto, we're not in Utah anymore.*

At last I reached the designated number on Durant. I found myself in front of a huge ungainly structure—a one-time Alpha Chi Omega sorority house gone to seed—where Hannah, according to her letters, resided with a number of roommates who were somehow deeply and crucially involved in making the planet a better place.

I stood out front for quite some time, with my backpack on and the wonderfully mixed Berkeley crowd, an astonishing blend of races, lifestyles, and wardrobes, streaming past me on the sidewalk, intent on countercultural errands. I had not called ahead; I did not know what to expect. It had been almost three years since I had seen Hannah by then.

At last I walked up the sidewalk and rang the bell. There was a long delay, during which I gathered from shouted remarks within that the occupants of the house were negotiating laconically with each other as to who should answer it. Then the heavy oak door swung open on a hinge that needed grease and Hannah herself stood before me in shorts and a tank top, her fine firm arms and legs tanned in February, her tiger gaze a fresh surprise, her indigo eyes a memory of the homeland.

She looked at my face, looked at my backpack, and looked back at my face. "Oh, Mason, I'm so sorry."

I suppose it was precisely the right thing to say, because I immediately began to cry.

—

I had arrived in California damaged and filled with self-contempt, pained by the fiasco with LeeAnne, my failures of normality in general, and a host of bad canvases, prepared to work off my sins like a Puritan in the new land. Naturally enough, the first thing Hannah did was get me stoned.

It amounted to an initiation of sorts—the household had a lofty sense of mythological mission—though it took place with remarkably little ceremony. My backpack was simply set aside in the entry hall (beside another backpack, I noted) as Hannah led me into the kitchen, a tremendous, high-ceilinged room, a relic of the house's sorority days, equipped to feed twenty. Here three of her housemates and the other new arrival were brewing up a pot of what turned out to be mushroom tea. I was introduced all around as Hannah's painter friend from Utah, which (especially the Utah part) I could see was going to take some living down.

The housemates themselves presented distinct types, variations on old themes in a West Coast key. Albert, whom Hannah alone called "Hal" and with whom I gathered she was sleeping, was from Colorado, a confident alpha male of twenty-five making every effort to soften the edges of an arrogance once destined—and possibly destined still—for Wall Street. Certainly his sleek blond ponytail seemed eminently detachable to me, as superfluous as an appendix. He had a newly minted M.B.A. from Cal–Berkeley, but sex, drugs, and the plight of the spotted owl had temporarily derailed his business career. Nothing, however, could have derailed his principled certitude: Albert's support for the old-growth redwoods somehow protruded even into our casual introductions. He spoke too softly, with what seemed to me an unsustainable mildness, and shook hands too limply—nonviolently, as it were, apparently according to notions of Saint Francis and Gandhi, who were also cited early. (Although I believe Saint Francis had a warm, firm grip.) I disliked Albert instantly, but perhaps that was simply because he was sleeping with Hannah.

As it turned out, he was also sleeping with Jarmine Key, the other woman in the kitchen. (Arriving at the Durant Street household was like tuning in to a particularly fervid soap opera in progress.) A distant relation of both F. Scott Fitzgerald and Francis Scott Key, Hannah said—as if this could help orient me—Jarmine was an elongated, unworldly brunette from the greater Chicago area with slightly startled pop-eyes and a bit of a stutter. She wore a long black dress like a Halloween witch's costume and seemed to be trying for a languid effect, but dozens of silver bracelets crashed and jangled up and down her skinny arms like loose equipment in the hold of a ship on a stormy sea. This constant metallic clatter gave Jarmine a slightly pell-mell air, a careening quality that, with her wide eyes and slightly horsey jaw, made me think of Ichabod Crane. The first thing she said to me was, "You seem *serene.*" I was not serene at all, of course; even more than usual I was one bad moment away from falling apart; but I smiled and nodded. I could see right away how important serenity was to Jarmine.

Brewing the mushroom tea at the stove, with an alchemical air, was the third housemate, Bobby Van Knott, a childlike wisp of a kid with straggly shoulder-length hair the color of weathered gold. He was barefoot in that tough easy way of the often-barefoot, a Huck Finn (he was actually from North Carolina and had a delightful, soft, incongruous drawl) replanted firmly on urban California ground. He had gathered the mushrooms himself, Hannah told me, with just a trace of awe. I smiled and nodded at this man-child, into whose shamanic hands we were all committing ourselves so blithely.

"Don't worry," the kid reassured me, reading my mind. "I test them all out on myself first. And *I'm* still alive. I think."

"We all trust Bobby," Hannah smiled.

"You 'think'?" I repeated uneasily.

"There are certain states of consciousness in which it's very hard to tell," he said, quite seriously, and mixed some spices into the pot of tea—vanilla, nutmeg, and a bit of cinnamon. Just like Mom used to make.

The last person present was a guest of Jarmine's, an old boyfriend of hers from high school named Mike. It was Mike whose backpack stood beside mine in the entryway. He had arrived by Greyhound from Chicago not half an hour before me, and much was made of the synchronicity, but I did not feel much needed to be made of it. Mike was a clean-cut young man terrorizing his parents by taking a semester off from Northwestern and he struck me as a little dazed by what had become of his prom date. His eyes tracked Jarmine's white arms through every jangling movement. Prepared to go gentle into that good night, but not quite sure what was asked of him, Mike spoke little, though he did mention that he had been reading Schopenhauer.

Van Knott hummed a little note; the tea was ready. The motley cups and mugs were filled, each in its turn. We drank without ceremony and sat around the table, self-consciously expectant, glancing at one another from time to time to see if anything wild had happened to anyone else. But no immediate effects were evident. Albert took the opportunity to harangue the captive audience further on the importance of stopping Georgia-Pacific in their tracks, but all my sympathy for the redwoods and the marbled murrelets could not make me like the man or find his self-righteousness anything but tedious. I kept glancing at Hannah, wondering how far she went with this strident stuff, but Hannah sat serenely, the clear high priestess of this household, taking it all in with a magnanimous air, her deep, dark eyes untroubled and cool. She winked at me once, but otherwise seemed inclined to let Hal have his way.

Three years had made her face a fresh mystery to me. I studied her obliquely while the rest of the group talked on about chaining themselves to trees and organizing letter-writing campaigns and what Saint Francis would have done in the face of Georgia-Pacific's rape of the ancient forests, and all at once Hannah's face turned into LeeAnne's.

"And then *I became a tree,*" Albert exulted abruptly.

I glanced at him to see if this was literally true and saw that it was not. But it seemed to be true of me—I could feel a sudden rootedness, and time had slowed to forest time. In the next year I might accumulate an eighth of an inch of new growth, one thin ring among hundreds, and no big deal at that: I was a redwood, all right, and this insufferable young man was all that stood between me and destruction.

"That's beautiful, Bertie," Hannah murmured, perhaps a little indulgently, like a mother to a child. Her face was her own again now, and radiant; the flash that had lit my broken heart had passed. I could no longer remember what Hannah was talking about—language itself was already becoming a sort of distraction by then—but all my nerve endings thrilled to the music of her voice. She smiled back at me across the table, a slow, knowing smile. It was possible for that moment to believe that it had all been a dream until that very moment. I had dozed, obviously, and was awakening only now. How else could I have forgotten what it meant to see her face?

On the wall behind Hannah, over the stove, the old AXΩ sorority logo glowed in golden letters on the greasy wood—the Alpha and the Omega, I realized, the secret of the universe, the beginning and the end. It had been here all along and its name was Love.

"It's so strange to be here," I marveled.

Hannah smiled again. "What's strange is to ever be anywhere else."

Through the rest of the afternoon and into the evening, the cosmos unfolded in all its vast magnificence and the kingdoms rose and fell. At some point Albert did in fact become a tree. We all did, briefly, and forests too, and whole ecosystems came and went on planets not yet born. "Schopenhauer was right!" Mike kept exclaiming. He had pulled volume two of *The World as Will and Representation* out of his backpack, where it had been stashed in an outer pocket for easy access like a tourist's guide to California; he kept thumbing through it, looking for the exact passage in which Schopenhauer had captured the essense of the universal process, until he freaked out and had to be put to bed by Jarmine. The jangle of Jarmine's bracelets as she led Mike off seemed to me as rich and lilting as the music of the spheres. I understood somehow that those bracelets had always spoken volumes and that it had been me who was deaf.

Meanwhile, Van Knott circulated through the house on subtle missions of his own, crossing the wood floor cautiously as if it were an exposed meadow and he were a deer or a hunter or something subject to ambush from the sky. He eventually made his way out into the backyard and disappeared into the vegetation.

Some time after darkness had fallen, I found myself alone in the kitchen, staring again at the Alpha and Omega through flame and smoke and trying to remember Everything. The flame was beneath the pan of leftover tea, the liquid portion of which had boiled away by then; the smoke was from the mushroom residue burning; and part of the Everything I was trying to remember was whether circumstances implied some activity on my part.

While I pondered this and other questions without arriving at any definite conclusions, Hannah hurried into the room and turned the stove off. I smiled at her gratefully, astounded at her deftness on the planet. Through all the vastness of the day's wild journeys, through every incarnation and every demise, through all the bardos and rebirths, Hannah had recurred, and every glimpse of her face had been like touching home.

"I don't see how you can think you know how you're going to die when there is no death," I told her, *de profundis*.

Hannah smiled at me sadly, indulgently, as she had smiled at Albert when he became a tree. She was an amazing woman, really—always one step ahead of the obvious mistakes being made at any point on the long and winding visionary road.

"There's death, Mason," she said, and hesitated delicately before addressing the real issue of the moment. She didn't want to hurt my feelings, but Albert, it seemed, was waiting upstairs …she was afraid that I expected…and I should know that she and Albert…and so forth.

I waved my hand; nothing was simpler; on the soul level everything worked out. The mushrooms did that much for me that night, at least: committed me to a wisdom beyond what I had actually attained. I had, of course, been hoping to sleep with her myself. Some part of me would always hope to sleep with Hannah, though I insist that sex was not, entirely, the point.

Hannah looked relieved. "You're an angel, Mason."

"Apparently."

She laughed. "Welcome to California. I'm glad you're here." Then she kissed me good night, like a sister, like a friend, as she would kiss me for years to come, and left me to my meditations.

Some time later Jarmine cycled through the kitchen briefly, dispatched by Hannah perhaps, jangling like a Hindu goddess with many arms. I was given to understand that there was a sexual option, and even that it would please everyone if I entered the complex house equation. But the rarity of redeeming beauty in a universe vast with suffering was upon me by then, and the opportunity passed—genially enough, as Jarmine went back to bed with Mike and gave him something to think about besides Schopenhauer. I sat alone at the kitchen table through most of the rest of that sleepless night, finding extraordinary things in the grain of the battered wood, trying to capture the poignancy of the beginning and the end as my sketchpad dissolved into its component molecules of bodiless bliss.

In retrospect, it is the middle to which I should probably have been paying attention. I woke from a brief doze near dawn surrounded by a scatter of genuinely incoherent abstractions, several erotic studies bordering on the lewd, one good sketch of Hannah, and the beginnings of a letter to LeeAnne; and it occurred to me, in the first bleak light of day, trying to recall what it was that had so possessed me in the greasy A and Ω on that greasy wall, that it was going to take longer to sort through California than I had thought.

I woke in blackness in the Golden Inn, briefly disoriented, a dream of Hannah seeping away. Sammy's breathing from the next bed was labored and uneven—he was dreaming too, it seemed. My own dream had been sweet and sad and beautiful, and as I lay there it seemed to me that I couldn't bear it.

There had been a time in my life when I would have taken that emotion to the streets and walked it off, walking the night away if necessary. Even now, had I been alone, I would have turned the light on and painted or sketched, if only for the sobering of failure and the remedy of work. But that was the last thing Sammy needed now, his father's lamp burning all night long through a poignancy attack. And so I lay still in the darkness and simply grieved, and I was afraid. Because I was losing it, it seemed to me: I was really losing it.

# a glimpse of the perseids

But some are twisted with the love
Of things irreconcilable,—
The slant moon with the slanting hill:
O Beauty's fool, though you have never
Seen them again, you won't forget.
Nor the Gods that danced before you
When your fingers spread among stars.

Hart Crane, "The Bridge of Estador"

*In the morning,* breakfast unexpectedly turned into an ordeal. I had not counted on the crowd, for one thing. It seemed that everyone in Golden was crammed into the placid little diner of the night before. The breakfast crowd in Golden was a rowdy one, and the cheerful din struck me as a kind of assault. I was already recognizing that my own reservoir of patience had run dry when Sammy rebelled at the inadequacy of the available cereals. He insisted that only Frosted Flakes would do.

The waitress, looking harried and a little disapproving, ran over the list again, more slowly, with a slight Sesame Street inflection, a noble performance under the circumstances; but Sammy shook his head fiercely, continuously, in vehement rejection of every option from Cheerios on down to Froot Loops.

He was sinking moment by moment into an obstinacy I recognized all too well, but I felt vaguely hampered in my response, hobbled by irrational parental guilt and the sense of a larger statement here. At home Sammy cheerfully ate the granola laced with fruit that LeeAnne served up to try to ease him away from the usual sugared American morning. It was only on his visits to Hannah, I knew, that Frosted Flakes had even been an option.

"Why don't you just get some corn flakes and we'll sugar them up?" I suggested shamelessly.

"No!" Sammy folded his arms. He was close to tears and furiously, hopelessly dug in. Amid the world's grim flux, Sammy had found a ground of solid truth at last, and the nations could align, the cities shatter, and civilizations rise and fall around his right to Frosted Flakes. *Hier stand ich; ich kann nichts anders.* You could nail it to the door of the Prairie Chicken Cafe.

The waitress glanced over her shoulder as the cook's bell rang; she had two orders up, another table was beckoning for coffee, and she had obviously made her own assessment of the depth of Sammy's resolve.

"Why don't I let the two of you work it out?" she said sweetly and bolted.

I took a breath. "I know this has all been hard on you, Sammy, but you're going to have to eat *something*. How about pancakes?"

Sam shook his head so hard his hair flopped; words no longer sufficed to communicate his resolve. We were drawing attention from nearby tables by now—a little whorl of difficulty in the Prairie Chicken's cheerful bedlam. I felt like a stumbling gymnast, or a pairs skater botching his half of a jump: The Nebraska judges were marking me way down.

"We've got a long day ahead of us," I offered. "How about some scrambled eggs?" No response. "Waffles? Some oatmeal?" And, trying at least for a smile, "How about a good stiff shot of Irish whiskey and some beer nuts, with a milk chaser?"

"I'm not going to eat *anything.*"

"You most certainly are."

"I most certainly am *not.*"

The waitress reappeared, looking wary. "Do you have any granola?" I asked her, growing a little arbitrary perhaps in my desperation.

*"I don't want granola!"* Sammy shouted. "I don't want *anything!"* And he threw down his napkin and stormed from the restaurant in his finest Hannah style.

I sighed, feeling my own night's bad sleep somewhere behind my eyes. Through most of my life I have chosen the indignities of art over the indignities of family: I have renounced, and avoided, and made all the ruinous, impoverishing, even inhuman moves that the canvas seemed to demand. Yet, in the end, I was blessed to suffer fatherhood anyway. God knows I haven't always suffered well.

"We're going through a bit of a family crisis," I told the waitress apologetically, and laid a five on the table, for my coffee and her trouble, before hurrying out after my furious son.

I'd forgotten how fast Sammy could move when he put his mind to it. He was a hundred yards up the street by the time I reached the sidewalk, heading east at a steady trot, his short legs pumping and his small head bobbing. It wasn't far in any direction to get out of Golden, and Sammy was well beyond the town limits by the time I caught him. He'd slowed to a walk by then and was breathing hard, but he forged on relentlessly, ignoring me, his flushed face turned to the hot morning sun. I walked beside him, panting and sweating myself, grateful at least that he'd stopped running.

Around here, land without a town on it went to corn; already we were amid the savaged stubble of the recently harvested fields. Crows tracked our progress from the roadside wires, and the occasional truck blasted past on the narrow two-lane highway. Five miles up the road in the direction we were heading, Hannah's van had crossed the line and found its violent rest, but I was not sure whether that was part of Sammy's fierce air of pilgrimage or not. Most likely he was just winging it. I'd seen him flee a dentist's office once in a similar fashion: He'd gone half a mile in a direction that led nowhere but to freedom from the drill. He was still trailing the white dentist's bib like a convict's shackle when I caught up with him that day. When I'd asked him where he was going, Sammy had simply shrugged, "Away," as Hannah in the snowy graveyard had said, "A song," as if I were an idiot to have to ask.

Between trucks, all was silence; the heavy air was already rippling over the asphalt, thick with heat. And all around us, to the horizon, the land had offered up its season's fruitfulness and rested in devastation, in burnt golden ruins.

We had walked perhaps half a mile, over the rise and out of sight of the town, when it seemed to me by Sammy's slightly sheepish air of self-consciousness that it might be time to speak at last. But I held off, as I had learned long ago to hold off with Hannah herself, until Sammy blurted, "It's like we're trying to act like nothing *happened.*"

*Ouch,* I thought, and walked in silence a moment before I answered. "Sammy, when something this big happens it can't change everything right away, the way that it seems it should. I mean, it *does* change everything, but it changes everything from the inside out. And meanwhile, everything just keeps going too."

Sammy was silent, his eyes fixed on his feet; but he was listening. I went on, "Our lives are never going to be the same. Even if they look the same, they're not going to be the same. But it takes a long time to see what that means—it's something that surprises you moment by moment. The world is going to show us different things now, because *we're* different. But meanwhile we still have to eat and sleep and take our baths and do our work, and even if we get so sad sometimes we don't want to eat and we sleep bad and we can't do our work, we still have to be kind. It's not that waitress's fault that Hannah died."

Sammy glanced at me, not quite showing amusement, but not entirely displeased with himself. Hannah too, of course, had loved to shock the bourgeoisie. I said sternly, "It's not funny, buster. She was just doing her job and you acted like a little shit."

"Well, what about you?" he exclaimed. "You're acting like a shit to Hannah. You're acting like nothing happened!"

"Nobody but me knows what Hannah means to me. Nobody but you is ever going to quite know what she is to you. Love means what it means. I'm talking about the way you treat people."

"You were going to make *me* eat some stupid cereal I didn't want!"

"Then we both messed up," I admitted, which is the best you can do when they nail you like that.

Sammy scuffed his sneaker at the asphalt disgustedly. We walked for a while without speaking. But at last he said, with an air of conceding ground, "Do you think I should go back and say I'm sorry?"

I smiled, relieved. "No sense making a bigger deal out of it than it was. I think she was just glad to see us go, to tell you the truth. She's probably seen worse." I laughed. "I'll tell you one thing: I bet they have Frosted Flakes, the next time we go in."

Sammy chuckled, then sobered. "I want to go back to where Hannah crashed," he said. "I want to leave some flowers."

I took a moment with that, astonished and humbled, as I often am by Sammy. Apparently he *had* known what road we were on. "Sure. That's a fine idea."

"And I'm not going to eat."

"Sammy, you can't stop eating."

"I *can*. I'm going to. I'm not going to eat until—" He hesitated, and I watched his face as his mind went up and out, groping after some extremity, looking for the place where a fast so deep could end. "Until it's *right,*" he said at last.

I suppose LeeAnne would have handled it differently and found the high road to adequate nutrition; I suppose a lot of excellent parents would have found a way to tease or gentle or reason the kid into eating; I suppose and suppose and suppose, but in the end I am the father Sammy got. The kid had his Gandhi face on anyway, and I couldn't think of a better time to let him taste, a little, what it meant to make a vow.

"Okay," I said. "And I won't eat until you do."

"Fine." Sammy smiled, resolved and content, and we turned to walk back to town, to get some flowers.

The day after my arrival in California, Bobby Van Knott brewed up another pot of mushroom tea, heavier on the cinnamon this time, with a twist of lemon, and everyone in the house except Mike and me relaunched themselves. I was impressed—astounded, even—by my new housemates' readiness to reascend to the fungal heights. The Berkeley veterans were like Sherpas of the psyche, adapted to atmospheres and precipices that left me gasping for air and longing for level earth. It turned out that I had arrived at a seasonal festival of sorts, and I would see no one at sea level for the two weeks Van Knott's stash of freshly harvested mushrooms lasted.

Mike spent three days more or less barricaded in Jarmine's room, filling his journal with wild speculative musings that eventually brought him round to Kant. He left on a bus for Chicago not long after that, holding a fat copy of the *Critique of Pure Reason* in his hand like a metaphysical paperweight, renewed in his resolve to pursue an academic career, reconciled to the loss of Jarmine, and seemingly glad just to have survived his little jaunt west.

For my part, I set up an easel in the house's sunny, south-facing breakfast nook, stretched a small canvas, and stared at it. I had a notion of doing the Alpha and the Omega in oils, I suppose, and for months after that I kept that easel up, stubbornly, like the British dressing for dinner in India. But the truth was that my raw sense of Californian reality did not lend itself to statements in oil at that point.

Meanwhile, I ended up doing a lot of watercolors of the stunning bougainvillea that framed the back porch steps, grateful for the sumptuous fuchsia-colored petals. I was content, if conscious of a pervasive incongruity, with the gentle wash of color seeping into spaces on the page. All around me Hannah and her housemates cavorted in vaster fields made Elysian by the seemingly bottomless pot of mushroom tea. The music alone could have sustained an altered state of consciousness, and I will never again hear certain works by Jethro Tull without a certain sense of nostalgia and cosmic isolation.

I missed LeeAnne desperately, missed the butter dish and the walks to the store, missed the perfect shape of her hand in mine and the perfect music of her laugh and the way she insisted on tucking in the quilt. I was disoriented and lonely and afraid already that California was too much for me, but from time to time Hannah would pass through my little de facto studio and I would take heart at the sight of her face.

"Are you okay?" she asked, the day after I arrived.

I just rolled my eyes. And we laughed. It was not necessary to be okay with Hannah, but it was necessary to retain your sense of humor.

Hannah settled in the stuffed chair opposite me, folding her legs up under her like a Buddha, a yoga trick she must have acquired in Berkeley. In the old days she would already have had her guitar out, but these were the new days: Hannah had been telling me in her letters for almost a year that there'd been way too much ego in her art. Putting the old Martin in a case amounted for her to a sort of transcendence. She was laying the foundations of a healthier civilization, and, as in all revolutions, decent art was the first thing to go.

We'd been arguing about this by mail for months, but I wasn't prepared to argue now. Instead, I showed her my ego-ridden paintings of bougainvillea blossoms. Hannah politely nodded at these, pronouncing them "Not bad," as symptoms of an elitist and patriarchal preoccupation went.

"So—" she said, handing the sketchbook back. "Are you here to stay?"

"I suppose I am."

"What happened?"

"LeeAnne wanted to have a baby."

"And a house with a white picket fence, I suppose?"

This was true, of course, but struck me as beside the point. "I think I chickened out."

"Or did her a favor."

Hannah meant, I knew, that both of us had been loosed into our broader, truer destinies. Certainly LeeAnne was free now to breed with more suitable stock, and I was free to pursue my unpopular art, but I could not possibly be wholly pleased by this. Looking at my sad, beautiful, useless little bougainvillea petals drying on the page, I could have wept. Ahead of me lay all the emptiness of California—a state unmarred, it seemed, by a single white, restrictive picket fence. We do scramble over such barriers at our peril.

Seeing how miserable I was, Hannah made a mournful noise of sympathy and reached to take my hand.

"Ah, Mason," she murmured affectionately.

"The thing is, I really would have liked to have been a better man."

"It's too late for that, I suppose." Hannah smiled, though I know she believed in her heart that California would make me one. But we all had to pass through the ruins of the self on the way to the new Jerusalem.

After that Hannah came by often to converse and cajole. I continued to believe in my old-fashioned way that I was a contemptible human being who had failed at everything he had touched, and she believed the world was dissolving into God even as we spoke and that angels walked among us, but a surprisingly large common ground existed between these views. On the best of days Albert would be off somewhere saving the trees and Hannah and I would sit for hours, talking about whatever came to mind, while the afternoon sunlight of Berkeley's astonishing February moved across the scuffed wood floor. The mushrooms remained a factor, to be sure, but, even stoned, Hannah was actually very lucid, and we had always talked well in any case.

I still could not look at her without longing. Hannah's skin, warm and golden, filled every silence for me; the jounce of her breasts beneath her T-shirt echoed through my days and nights. We had agreed that sex was not in the cards—or in the stars, as Hannah's new enthusiasm for the relevance of the planets would have it—but our reasoned agreement ran far ahead of my visceral reality, and my heart's ache. Her scent, or an unexpected angle of her neck, could make me nuts.

The truth of the shift seemed indisputable. Something in Hannah had genuinely moved on. And something in me had stayed, somewhere, somehow—with LeeAnne, perhaps (Hannah felt, for instance, that I should remove my wedding ring, which I stubbornly continued to flaunt, like a war wound), or with the old, bounded world of the canvas. The specifics hardly mattered. She wasn't playing the guitar anymore either, Hannah would point out when we discussed the situation—which we did often enough, at length, almost luxuriously. What mattered was *letting go.*

I took these discussions as a form of sublimation. We talked about relationships, endlessly—hers with Albert, mine with LeeAnne. We talked about the spiritual path (mine seemingly dead-ended, hers branching like the evolutionary tree). And all the while I sharpened my need against the stone of our chaste new reality.

One afternoon, we crossed the Bay to San Francisco to see a revival of *Casablanca* at a little art house in the Richmond district, and I astonished myself by weeping at Humphrey Bogart's nobility on the airport tarmac. I had been craving an image of meaningful renunciation and as we came out of the theater at dusk I was speechless with a vision I had not, perhaps, quite earned. The street seemed new, washed clean by art's superior reality. Hannah wanted a cigarette, in utter contradiction to her Californian commitment to purity, which indicated to me that she was moved as well. We stopped at a corner store and bought a pack of Virginia Slims.

Hannah lit up, cupping the match expertly against the breeze. She had learned to smoke in junior high and could still look very cool with a cigarette in her hand. "I'm not ready to get on a bus yet, are you?"

"Actually, I have this strange urge to go join the Free French forces in Tangiers. Or at least to paint Moroccan landscapes."

Hannah smiled indulgently and blew three perfect smoke rings. "Let's walk back through the Presidio. We can catch a bus in the Marina."

"Sounds good."

We walked up the street, through the gates of the old army base and into the eucalyptus groves. The fog was coming in, turning the evening drizzly. I was still burning inside with that pained, clear light I'd crawl on glass to keep, but which never stays.

The foghorns moaned. We took an obscure path through the darkening woods, breathing in the smell of wet eucalyptus, until we stumbled abruptly into deep sand amid a grove of uprooted trees. Massive trunks lay everywhere, blown down by a recent windstorm, their shallow roots torn right out of the earth.

"It's like a burial ground," Hannah whispered, lowering her voice instinctively, and I nodded my silent agreement.

We moved through the deep, damp sand, in the twilight, to where the particularly massive carcass of a tree lay like an ancient beast, gray in weird decay. It gave us pause enough that magic came; we stood together beside the hulk and Hannah surprised me by raising her arms, in spontaneous invocation. Close by on the Bay, the foghorn blew, and a silence settled on the ravaged grove. Above us the sky streamed, the fog blowing past at treetop level.

We walked on without a word as darkness settled in the woods. By now I had only the vaguest sense of where we were going, but I was deeply content. The jagged sense of urgency that had tormented me for months had passed: I wanted only what I had, and what I had seemed precious.

Just when it seemed that we were lost, a single streetlight up ahead made the night fog real. Hannah and I walked toward the blurry light, through black trees creaking in the thick wind from the sea. The sky had settled by now, holding the orange glow from the city so close that it seemed to light our way. I felt purged of hurt and need, for that moment, buoyed in the night's hush. I felt that love was possible to me again, and that I welcomed whatever form it took. It was just so sweet to be alive.

The streetlight was at a bus stop, where the forest path crossed a road. Hannah and I looked at each other for a moment and smiled, almost ruefully. It was the sort of moment that once upon a time would have led to bed. Then she took my arm, tenderly, and we walked on along the road, in the deepening dark, to the next light up ahead.

I slept on an old army cot in an attic room too small to be a bedroom and too large to be a closet, and continued to paint in what everyone with charming anachronism called the breakfast nook (the niche had not seen a breakfast, I was sure, since the place was built); and in general I was integrated into the sprawling Durant Street household with remarkably little fuss. Albert postured a little, to be sure, and called for a vote at the next house meeting to determine whether I should be allowed to stay, but even he voted me okay when the hands went up. I got a job at a nearby taqueria and spent my afternoons skidding on the lard-slick floor amid the heat and the sizzle of frying chicken, cooking pot after pot of beans and chopping the onions and tomatoes for their potent salsa. This enabled me to pay my share of the rent, an apparently novel idea which astounded everyone at Durant Street almost as much as what they saw as the weird discipline of my painterly mornings. But they were prepared to be compassionate with me in my backwardness and fear of divine Reality. I had, after all, just arrived from Utah.

In a spirit of initiation, Bobby Van Knott conducted me to several Grateful Dead shows at the nearby Greek Amphitheater, instructing me earnestly on how to find God between the notes in the extended drum solo. Through the grace of the

Lord and a certain amount of marijuana smoke I did perceive that God was there. Jarmine took me to her Wednesday night Sufi group, where her teacher taught a sort of spinning dance that Jarmine said made you disappear—so casually did we all embrace annihilation then. I went and spun and sure enough learned to find the still point at the center while the world around me blurred away and my solidity dissolved into perfect silence and everything became a single blurring stream of Love; and afterward Jarmine and I had coffee. I was becoming very fond of her and found her jangle soothing, though I continued to avoid falling into bed with her.

Albert, blessedly, ignored me for the most part, while Hannah herself saw to it that I did not neglect my public responsibilities in the midst of spiritual expansion. Several times during this period we carpooled out to the nuclear weapons laboratories in Livermore and sat down in the road with a few hundred other people to keep the world safe for flowers and children. I spent three days in jail eating army-surplus spaghetti and franks off paper plates with Daniel Ellsberg and Wavy Gravy, and eventually we all pled no contest to misdemeanor traffic violations in the service of humanity. "Love is the only law," Hannah told the judge, who nodded, perhaps a little wearily, and sentenced us to time served and the minimum fine, suspended.

One night, the second summer after I had settled in Berkeley, Hannah and I were sitting on the broad, flat, tar-and-gravel roof of the Alpha Chi Omega house, drinking cheap white wine out of a gallon jug. Above us, the Perseid meteor shower was making its annual show with a certain poignancy (I had always watched it in Utah with LeeAnne). Hannah and I had positioned ourselves in two lawn chairs, facing north, with the wine between us. Beyond the city's glow, in the sky near Andromeda, the occasional bit of busted comet made its thrilling silent sizzle and dissolved.

We sat for a long time in a contented silence broken only by intermittent "oohs" and "ahhs" and the gurgling of the wine jug. At some point Hannah reached over and took my hand. Her fingertips were as soft as a baby's skin; her wonderful old Martin guitar remained in the closet, as it had since my arrival, and she had lost all her callouses. Hannah at this point believed her music had been a phase, and even an embarrassing one, like teenager poetry—something she had done to please people, or to posture.

"So have you given up on music entirely?" I asked, in the broad, honest, slightly drunken mellowness of the moment.

Hannah shrugged. "Maybe music's given up on me."

"Not likely."

"I was never as good as you thought I was, Mason."

"Hah."

She laughed. "It's really not that big a deal, sweetheart. Believe it or not, there are more important things in life."

"I don't think so."

"The sky at night. A loving friend. The beauty all around us."

I hesitated, then let it go. After a year and a half in California, I was feeling the first ease of an unexpected healing. Time and circumstances had worked their unforeseeable alchemy, and Hannah and I had found our way, almost in spite of ourselves, into friendship. I was even prepared by then to consider the possibility that Hannah had gone a bit beyond me into wisdom, while I languished in a facile art. Certainly I was content for that rare and precious moment to be holding her hand in the balmy August air, marveling at what life had brought us to, and wondering, with a pain that finally seemed manageable, whether LeeAnne, in Utah, was looking up as well.

And so I held my tongue. Above us, the night sky, lit with the steady distant violence of burning stars, dwarfed music and love and watercolors alike; and every once in a while a long-forgotten piece of some ancient wandering thing flared briefly in the darkness near Perseus and Andromeda, ending its ancient wandering in flame.

—

In Golden, Sammy and I found a bright little flower shop on Main Street. I slipped him a twenty-dollar bill as we went in, and Sammy chose Hannah's bouquet flower by flower, somber and self-conscious and determined to spend every penny. He stopped every few minutes to recalculate the cost of the accumulating irises, lilies, and roses, lingering over the luxury of a bird of paradise, and agonizing over daffodils. He had a wonderful eye, and the final arrangement was spectacular. The woman who ran the shop, a pleasantly taciturn, silver-haired matron in jeans, running shoes, and a T-shirt that read "Stella's Flower Palace, Golden, NE," had somehow figured out what was going on. When the total came to $23.08, she hit one more button and took Sammy's twenty without a word.

We made the ten-minute drive to the accident site in silence. Everything looked different to me, going east, and I almost drove right past the spot. But Sammy declared, abruptly, *"Here."*

I pulled over and we got out of the car. Sure enough, glass on the shoulder crunched beneath our feet. Otherwise, there was little evidence of the crash. Sammy laid the bouquet on the little patch of scorched grass by the ditch, and we stood for a moment in silence, my hand resting on his shoulder.

The scene was oddly tranquil; Sammy's resolve had cleared a space for peace and I had a sense of pausing, however briefly, in my hectic course. For the first time since I'd heard the news, the world grew still and calm and lovely, and I remembered how I loved the woman who had died here, who had given me this son.

A mile away—two miles, even three—a truck was coming east. I watched it all the way, for what seemed like five or ten minutes, tracking the approach with a weird fascination. At last it blasted past and we flinched in its rough, hot wake. The flowers rolled twice, and a paper cup blew past.

Sammy waited for the air to settle, then walked back to the car. I followed, as I had so often followed Hannah, moved and a little uncomprehending.

Back in the motel room, Sammy lay down on the bed as soon as we came in, looking flushed and spent. I fetched a soda from the machine down the hall and poured it over some ice, and he drank gratefully from the plastic cup. Apparently his fast did not extend to Mountain Dew. I resolved to get us some fruit juice at the first opportunity.

While he rested, I went down into the lobby to the pay phone to make a call that seemed better made alone. Harmon Tulliver, of Tulliver's Funeral Home in Golden, answered on the first ring, as if he had nothing better to do. I suppose the clean-living populace of Golden were a healthy lot.

"Ah, yes, Mr. Mason, so glad you called. I'm sorry I wasn't able to get in touch with you earlier."

"We were out."

"I'm sure you're very busy, and sadly so. It *is* rather a mess, isn't it?"

The note was wholly wrong, but I was prepared to see it as one of the strange forms condolence took in the Midwest. "I suppose it is. Have you been able to—um—"

My sentence trailed off; it seemed too brutal to be so bare and businesslike, and I was looking for help. But Tulliver just prompted, as if I might have called about any number of things, "Yes?"

"The cremation, for God's sake. Has it been done?"

"Ah!" he exclaimed. "You don't know, then."

"'Know'?"

"I was served with a temporary restraining order this morning, Mr. Mason. It seems that Miss Johnson's father got a federal judge out of bed in the middle of the night. I am forbidden to perform the cremation and have been instructed to prepare the body for transport to New York."

"You didn't perform the cremation?" I said stupidly, unable to grasp it at once.

"I am forbidden to, Mr. Mason. By a federal judge. And, it would seem, by the victim's father."

I heard the reproach in his tone; he seemed to feel that I had tried to put something over on him. But I just said, "Can he *do* that?"

"Apparently he has, sir."

"So you were trying to contact me—"

"Well, obviously, to coordinate the, um, shipping arrangements. I assume you'll be accompanying the body?"

The image of Hannah's half-burned corpse flashed before me. Dazed as I was, I could appreciate the irony: After years of arguing with her about it, all I really wanted to do, at this point, was finish the fire's work. But it appeared I would not be able to do that in Nebraska.

"I suppose I will," I said resignedly, and we began to discuss the arrangements.

## eleven

## connection in chicago

There's always another death to die
Beyond the death you know,
Always another door of scars
To open to another room.

Rumi

—

**Things moved fast** for a while then, as things move fast in the worst of dreams. I called George Johnson's office immediately after my conversation with Tulliver and was expertly stymied by his secretary, who informed me that I had a date in a New York City courtroom in two days. At that time the judge who had issued the restraining order would decide on "the ultimate disposal of the remains."

"I'm sure he will," I said, and hung up feeling like a chess player caught by a particularly neat knight's fork. But there was nothing to do but play it out. I had my own relationship with the remains.

The train on which George Johnson had reserved passage for his daughter's body left Omaha at two that same afternoon. Johnson had purchased one of Tulliver's best caskets for what Golden's funeral-home director persisted in calling "shipment." I saw the box loaded from the baggage platform in the Omaha station, a lustrous, polished, pale cherrywood thing with big-knobbed gold handles, straight out of Hannah's worst nightmare of posthumous treatment. She was going out in style, in spite of her best efforts.

Tulliver, who was also there to see his shipment off (whether by court order or not I never knew), showed me how to work the casket's lock and, after a moment of hesitation that embarrassed both of us, gave me a copy of the key. A kind, awkwardly well-intentioned man with eyes the color of turkey gravy and a shining pate combed over with three strands of black hair, he clearly was not sure where right lay amid all this confusion, but he tended to believe it did not rest with me.

Sam impassively watched this farce unfold. I wondered what he made of it all. For his sake, I was minimizing my sense of outrage at the change of plans, conceding only that his grandfather and I were going to have to discuss the arrangements, but no doubt the kid had the basic picture. All the way from California to Nebraska, I had briefed him by easy stages on Hannah's desire for cremation and scattering to the wind, and it wasn't like *she* had changed her mind.

I had hoped there would be time to call LeeAnne, but we'd arrived at the station with minutes to spare. We boarded and found seats as the train began to move. Sammy settled in at once with his keyboard and headphones, like a commuter with a laptop, and passed into the inscrutability of his silent music. He was quieter even than usual, perhaps from low blood sugar. He hadn't eaten since dinner the night before.

I was ravenously hungry myself. I leaned back and looked out the window as the train ran past the stockyards toward the Missouri River, trying not to think about food. If you weren't playing gigs at every roadside bar and club that would let you set up your amps, it was eight short hours back to Chicago by way of Des Moines and Davenport, Iowa; and, after a change of trains, it was sixteen hours more from Chicago to New York.

Two years after I settled into the Durant Street house, Albert learned of an obscure species of clover that survived only on two hills in rural Marin County near Inverness. The newsletter in which he read of the clover's plight also mentioned that the land was for sale and in danger of development. The Western Kundalee Clover *(Trifolium obscurus)* lacked the glamour of the redwoods, but its plight was more desperate and we had been talking for some time now of the need to do something "in our watershed." Inverness was not actually *in* our watershed, but it was close enough, and the price was right, as grand gestures went. One thing led to another and, after a series of house meetings, we decided to buy the land ourselves and create a clover-friendly microcosm of the new society there.

Bobby Van Knott's grandfather had recently left him forty thousand dollars, so we were able to make a down payment on the land and pour the concrete foundations of a six-bedroom house immediately. (I do not recall anyone having been troubled by the incongruity of our eagerness to build in the heart of the clover's last refuge.) We devoted every weekend that summer to a comedy of amateur construction work.

These were delightful days, at least at first. Hannah in her toolbelt and sleeveless T-shirt was a wonder. She had been craving a big project to sink her teeth into for quite a while, and clearly was glad to have a hammer in her hands. She was the best carpenter among us, by far, the only one who could read a blueprint, the handiest with a power saw, and the hardest worker. Just watching her walk along a narrow scaffold plank, tanned and cocky and shiny with sweat, with a big piece of plywood balanced on her head, filled me with joy.

We would work all day in the sun and drink beer and eat campfire spaghetti at night. Looking up at the clear stars, we would congratulate each other on finally getting out of the city, but we had not counted the cost and the project stalled for lack of funds not long after the rainy season began in November. We had hoped to at least have the roof on by then, but had managed only the house's enormous skeletal frame, which visibly swayed in the wind as the first storm rolled in from Alaska just before Thanksgiving. The original population of sixteen Kundalee Clover plants under our stewardship was down to twelve by then. We had managed to back a truck over one patch of the precious things, which looked a lot like weeds in their dull nonflowering phase.

LeeAnne arrived in California that same December, ostensibly to continue her graduate studies in psychiatry at UCSF. She was still trying to keep her Freudian orthodoxy together at that point, but she had begun to read Jung. We had lunch in downtown San Francisco not long after her arrival and the first thing I noticed was that she was still wearing her wedding ring. LeeAnne and I had kept a wary connection alive by mail for years, in part by continually negotiating our divorce, but neither of us had ever managed to sign a paper.

"I keep meaning to take mine off," LeeAnne said, noticing my glance at the ring.

"Me too."

We sat for a moment in silence. The waiter arrived with our wine, a good Sonoma Chardonnay that glinted pale gold, like LeeAnne's hair, in the weak December sunlight. Our eyes met across the table, ruefully, humorously. I found my hand wanting to trace the line of her cheekbone, over to the ear and down, seeking the hollow of her throat like water in a dry stream bed.

"Ah, Jerry." LeeAnne shook her head, not without affection. "We never had a clue."

We drank to that. It was all much easier than we both had feared—even injured love does its own deep work in mystery over the course of years, whatever else we think is going on. LeeAnne and I caught up on the basic headlines of our lives over salad, and after lunch we walked up Van Ness together to take in the Klee show at the Museum of Modern Art. I'd been meaning to get downtown to see the exhibition for months, but with all the construction work in Inverness and the general spiritual hubbub, this was the first chance I'd had.

As we strolled through the rooms full of sketches, paintings, and lithographs, I could feel my eye coming alive; Klee's offhand ease at conjuring spontaneous form struck me with the force of revelation. Everywhere, his textured depths yielded up their deft surprises. I finally stopped in front of a little lithograph of a whimsical angel bringing some poor guy his breakfast and started copying it in pencil onto a blank spot on my gallery map, just to stay oriented amid the sudden expanses of vision. It seemed to me in that moment that it had been forever since I had seen something fresh.

LeeAnne circled the room and ended beside me.

"Klee always makes me feel like I never touched a pencil before and just learned that it's possible to draw," I told her.

LeeAnne smiled, just short of indulgent, a woman with her wits about her.

"I suppose it's always a blessing to begin again," she said.

It was dark by the time I got back to the Durant Street house, but no one else was home. Hannah, Albert, Bobby, and Jarmine had gone off that morning with a load of used bricks for the site in Inverness and were not back yet. I went at once into my studio space in the breakfast nook, where the canvas I had stretched for the Alpha and the Omega still stood on its easel in the corner like a plow rusting in an abandoned field. I'd ridden the train home after my afternoon with LeeAnne and

Klee, nursing a new notion of something delicate in acrylics—
an obliquity, part bird, part sky, part laughter. Miraculously, the
canvas looked like a live space again.

I had just started seeding the white with pencil strokes,
working from the sketches I had made on the train in the mar-
gins of my gallery map, when the others arrived home.

I could tell at once by the sullen silence that the day had not
gone well—everyone scattered at once to their separate rooms
without a word. Someone stomped into the kitchen. I heard
the refrigerator door open and a moment later Hannah
appeared in the doorway with two bottles of beer, looking
dirty, damp, and exhausted. She handed me one of the beers
and sank into the chair in the corner. Her jeans and boots were
caked with mud; her T-shirt, once white, was delicate orange.
(Jarmine had recently come under the influence of the guru
Rajneesh and switched her entire wardrobe to orange, and the
inevitable laundry mishaps had turned most of the rest of the
household's sheets, shirts, and underwear orange as well, making dilute disciples of us all.)

"God, what a day," Hannah sighed. "Never haul bricks with
hippies, Mason."

"Amen." I tapped her bottle with mine and we drank.

"*Crumbly* bricks, at that," Hannah continued, wiping her
mouth with the back of her hand. "They saw Albert coming
at the supply place, I guess—we got half a ton of the damned
things all the way up there, started unloading, and found out
that half of them are worthless. *Plus* we killed another clover.
Somebody just *stepped* on it—nothing left but a bootprint.
Can you believe it?"

"I'm just glad it wasn't me this time, to tell you the truth. I can't handle any more guilt over those damned clovers."

"Bobby started crying. He said he could hear it scream."

I laughed. "He's a sensitive guy."

"He's sensitive like a goddamned compass in a magnet store," Hannah said. "He was blasted on mushrooms all day long, going through some birth-and-death sequence in another galaxy. He probably stepped on the damn thing himself." She noticed the canvas for the first time. "My God, Mason, are you doing something there?"

"I've got half a notion," I conceded. "I'm under the influence of Klee, I should probably be locked up until I'm sober. But it's the first thing I've seen since I got to California that wasn't a watercolor or *Apocalypse Now,* so I thought I'd see what came of it."

"In oils?"

"Acrylics, I think. It's easier to clean up."

Hannah groaned. "I can see it's going to be hell to get you to pick up a hammer again."

"Or a brick."

She smiled, with an effort, unhappily. It could not please her to see me defect from the new society. Still, I felt that I had to be frank.

"I had lunch with LeeAnne today."

Hannah looked startled, then summoned a supportive expression. "No kidding? How did it go?"

"Really well, I think. It was wonderful to see her. We got sloshed to the brink of forgiveness on wine and salad, walked up to the Klee show afterward, and then had ice cream. Can you believe it, she's still wearing her wedding ring."

"Ah," Hannah murmured ambiguously. She had been telling me for years by now that wearing mine was holding my spirit back, that I had to forgive and let go and move on—Hannah's personal speciality.

We were silent a moment. Hannah took a long pull on her beer and finished it off, then looked at the empty bottle in mock surprise, as if it had betrayed her.

"I'm buying this round," I said quickly, and went to the kitchen to fetch us fresh bottles.

When I came back, Hannah had risen and was standing by the big picture window, looking out into the darkness of the backyard. I handed her her beer. She met my eyes and I saw, to my relief, that we were going to be all right. We raised our bottles to each other in a silent, slightly rueful toast. Then Hannah looked back out into the night.

After a moment, she offered, seemingly out of the blue, "I called my father this morning."

Her tone was hard to read. I replied, cautiously, "Oh?"

"Yeah. Albert's been pestering me for weeks to ask Dad to give me a loan, for this construction."

I groaned sympathetically. "How remarkably awkward."

"You have no idea." She glanced at me. "They'd just gotten back from the hospital and were about to call *me*. My mother's got some kind of tumor in her left breast—the doctors want to operate right away."

"Oh, Hannah..."

"They're not sure whether it's malignant or not, but she'll probably lose the breast, at least. My father wants me to come back right away." She laughed unhappily. "He wants me to play Vivaldi for her."

"Vivaldi?"

"The adagio movement of the guitar sonata in B minor, among other things. My mother loves it. The family myth is that we all used to sit around in perfect bliss when I was sixteen and would play it at Christmas. In my father's movie, I go back and play it in the hospital room, post-op, and everything is fine again."

"And?"

"I told him I had to get a roof on this damned house before all the flooring warps," Hannah snapped, but the defiance quavered a little at the end. She looked down at her beer bottle. Her hands, I noted, were dirty and battered, bloodied from handling bricks all day. It had been a point of pride with Hannah for some time to offer those exquisite instruments to the construction process, but it pained me suddenly beyond endurance.

"Let's get you cleaned up, for God's sake," I said, and led her like a child to the bathroom, where Hannah suffered me to gently wash her hands. I soaped and scrubbed and rinsed, applied antiseptic, and bandaged the torn skin; then, on a tender impulse, kissed her knuckle. Hannah surprised me by beginning to cry. As the tears spilled over and down her cheeks, she turned her head into my shoulder. I put my arm around her and for some time we sat on the edge of the bathtub without speaking.

At last Hannah snuffled, reached for a Kleenex, and blew her nose.

"Do you know— " she marveled, "When I got off the phone and told Albert about the conversation with my father, about my mother, all Albert said was, 'Does that mean he's not going to give you the loan?'"

I didn't know what to say.

"Oh yes, the new society is a lovely thing indeed." Hannah shook her head. "God, Mason, what have we come to?"

"I don't know," I said, and kissed her battered hand again.

That night, Hannah went up to her room and took her old Martin out of the closet. For the next two weeks she played the Vivaldi sonata over and over again, until her fingers bled, laboring to get it right. When she had it down flawlessly, she made an audio tape, tacked on a nasty, rollicking rendition of "Friend of the Devil," and fired it off to her family in a Christmas card.

That might have been the end of it, except that by return mail a Christmas card arrived from George Johnson, along with a check for $53,200. I have no idea how he arrived at that particular figure. On the memo line of the check, it read simply, "loan."

Hannah, furious, would have torn the check in half, but Albert stopped her.

"We can't afford a gesture like that when there's so much work to do for the good of the planet," he declared.

Hannah looked at him, and I saw the end of their relationship in her eyes. But all she said was, "Yes, I suppose you're right." The money went nobly for a roof and walls on the Inverness villa, and paid off the balance on the land. Still, I don't think Hannah's heart was ever in it after that.

I finally managed to reach LeeAnne during our brief layover in the train station in Chicago. While Sammy sipped an orange juice out of earshot and monitored the departures board, I tried to explain to my wife how necessary it was that I go to New York and do battle with George Johnson over his desire to bury his daughter in a decent and traditional way.

"Uh-huh." LeeAnne sounded dubious.

"I promised her. She was terrified of having a funeral like her mother's."

"You told me once that her playing at her mother's funeral was one of the most beautiful things you'd ever heard."

"It was poignant," I conceded. "She transformed the moment, once she was backed into a corner."

"Well?"

"Well, it's not like you can count on *that.*"

LeeAnne was silent, rather pointedly.

*"What?"* I said.

"If what you had with Hannah meant anything, I don't see how you can count on anything *else.*"

A man with a shiny leather briefcase was hovering nearby,

waiting impatiently to use the phone. I held up one finger placatingly, and told LeeAnne, "That may be too deep for me. I think I just need something simple and petty."

"You know you don't believe that."

"You're saying I should just turn the other cheek? Let the dead bury the dead?"

"I'm saying that maybe you should ask yourself again what love really requires of you here."

"You're saying to behave myself. And so she loses. And everything she did was a little shadow play for children, and what it meant to her was a dream, and none of it has anything to do with the real world, which goes on and on and grinds us all to dust. And forget art, and forget music, and forget the glimpse of something lovely that made her offer her whole life up—"

The man with the briefcase gave up in disgust and headed off to find another phone. LeeAnne exclaimed, exasperated, "Do you really think you're going to validate Hannah's life by having her cremated instead of buried? By throwing her last bit of spite in her father's face? It's the worst kind of idolatry, Jeremiah; it's the letter of the law."

"That's not the point. The technicalities don't matter. The point is that Hannah had the courage to stick her neck out for what she believed, her whole life. And she asked me to do the same for her, when the moment came, for the sake of what we shared. That's what I'm doing. That's *all* I'm doing. And I'm willing to be an ass for that."

"I can see that you are."

LeeAnne's tone was unassailably dry. We were silent.

"And Sammy?" she asked at last.

"He threw a fit at breakfast," I conceded. "But then he bought flowers, his idea, and we took them out to the crash site. It was a good moment, actually."

"There's your real ceremony right there, then. The rest of this is nonsense. Let Mr. Johnson have what's left."

I ignored that, for the moment. "Sam's got himself on some kind of hunger strike," I said, though I had not intended to tell her. But she was the only one I could tell. "A fast."

"He's not eating?"

"Not until it's *right,* he says. It's all very solemn."

"Oh, Jerry. Since when?"

"All day, so far."

LeeAnne was silent. The station loudspeaker blared unintelligibly, announcing a departure. I caught Sammy's eye across the floor—he has a much better ear than I do—and he shook his head. Not our train.

"He seems okay," I offered to LeeAnne. "It's his way of saying this is important. I think he felt like I was taking the whole thing too lightly."

LeeAnne laughed, surprising me. "He's certainly the only one who would think *that.* You're insane, both of you."

"I suppose we are," I said, pleased.

"Try not to let him waste away entirely, Jerry."

It was as close to a blessing as I had a right to expect, and I felt a rush of warmth for her. "I love you, LeeAnne."

"What luck. Because I'm way out on a limb here, I'm

knocked up and down on my luck and I've been hoping you'll make an honest woman of me."

Again the loudspeaker blared, and this time Sammy got to his feet. "I made an honest woman of you years ago, sweetheart. The real problem has been making an honest man of me."

"You got *that* right."

"They just called our train, I'm afraid."

"Just when you were starting to make sense....Oh, hey!" LeeAnne exclaimed. "I almost forgot—that guy came by the studio yesterday. The one who was going to pick out a painting?"

"Don't tell me he actually bought something."

"He bought three."

"No!"

"One of the recent landscapes; and something sort of abstract called *Into the City;* and an early thing, *Burning Music* number something-something."

"Number what?"

"Seventeen, I think."

I let a moment pass, then said, "Number Seventeen is not for sale."

"Oh, *Jerry.*"

"It's not that big a deal. There are just certain things I'd rather not see hung on the wrong wall, in the wrong light, beside a poster for Disneyland or an Andy Warhol print, or behind a potted plant. Tell him he can pick out anything else he wants, give him three for the price of two."

"Tell him yourself, sweetheart. He already hauled them off and left a check."

I said nothing, stubbornly.

"Look, Jerry, I know the timing is bad. But it's all part of learning to let things go. You offer something up, you've got to be prepared for the world to take it."

"Give me his number, I'll call him myself."

She sighed, and obliged. I folded the piece of paper and put it in my pocket. We were silent a moment. Sammy was making urgent gestures by now, and I nodded at him.

"I really do have to go."

"Of course you do," she said.

I would rather have missed the train than hung up on that note. "What?"

"Nothing. *Everything.*" LeeAnne hesitated. "Look, Jerry, just call me when it's over, okay?"

"LeeAnne—"

"I'm serious. Tell me when your flight gets in, whether it's in a day or a week or a month, and I'll meet you at the airport. Tell me then if I still have a son or if you let him starve to death on some razor edge of scruple. Tell me then if we still have a *marriage*. But I don't think I can stand the blow-by-blow of your noble struggle with poor George Johnson. I don't think I really care to follow every twist and turn of the fight over the remains."

"Lee*Anne*—"

"The funniest thing of all is, you're just like him. You're both stupid with love for Hannah, and yet all either of you can do is read the fine print on the contract and look for the legal leverage and hang on too tight to things you should have learned to let go of long ago. You're two of a kind and you deserve each other. But Hannah deserves better."

"God knows that's true," I said, but LeeAnne had already hung up. It felt like hell, but I had to get moving. Sammy was tugging at our big suitcase like an ant with a grain of rice, and we had a real run, by then, to make our train.

## twelve

## such a simple thing

Asceticism is a mistake
sought out suffering is a mistake
but what comes to you free is enlightening.

Agnes Martin

---

*Through the night,* as the train took us east through Toledo, Cleveland, and Youngstown, Sammy slept on the seat opposite me, my jacket draped over him. I alternately dozed and reviewed Hannah's will. The last page of addenda had been written after her mother's funeral, a high Catholic affair and a disaster of sorts, marred by a sleety snowstorm and the cumulative strain of unnatural civility among the survivors. Hannah, who had already made several trips back while her mother was still alive, made me fly back to New York with her for the funeral, insisting that she couldn't go alone. In the shock of her loss, she didn't trust herself to behave well on her own.

George Johnson had met us at the airport, so genuinely undone that not even his daughter could find it in her heart to treat him badly, at least not at first. For once we all made conversation and did our best to muddle through gracefully, and for a time we succeeded.

On the day of the service, though, the roads had frozen into black treachery and mourners' fenders crumpled left and right. According to George Johnson, it had been Arlene's wish that her daughter would play at her funeral mass, but he had neglected to inform Hannah of this until the morning of the service, long after the programs had been printed up. (He later said he had been afraid to ask her sooner, for fear she would say no.) A fuming Hannah, caught off-guard and unprepared, had obliged him with a rending instrumental version of Dylan's "One More Cup of Coffee for the Road," which everyone mistook for a gypsy dirge, and the adagio movement from Vivaldi's guitar sonata in B minor, her mother's favorite from the days when they had all hoped Hannah would go to Juilliard.

Then, playing on her first guitar, retrieved from the closet of her childood for the occasion, Hannah had finished off the set defiantly by singing "Hell and Back (A Walk in the Blinding Light)," transposed on the spot to a minor key.

> *I've done the crucifixion, babe—*
> *I've done the little hell—*

I had winced as I recognized the first notes; it had seemed an outrageous choice under the circumstances, but Hannah pulled it off beautifully. I don't think I'd realized until that day how much love and forgiveness was in that song. Hannah's anger at being put on the spot had been tamed by then to a hard blue flame like the tip of a focused blowtorch and her voice warmed the church, building like a slow fire until its quiet exaltation blazed at the lightest touch of breath.

Looking around the chilly, crowded room, I saw the matrons dabbing at their eyes. I was sure most of them hadn't cried at a folk song since Ed Ames sang "They Call the Wind Mariah." But for a moment everyone was young again. Hannah looked like her mother, they had all said afterward; and Arlene, at the front of the church choir, had always looked like an angel.

Even Hannah's father's eyes had grown moist, though later, on the way to the cemetery, he could not refrain from an awkward joke about the rustiness of the Vivaldi.

His daughter had just smiled at him, her deadly tiger smile, which she always told me she had gotten from her mother, though I never found it in a single photograph of Arlene.

"Ah, Daddy, Daddy, Daddy," she had said. "If only you could have learned a single thing, somewhere along the way."

*It can't be the usual thing,* Hannah had written in 1985, revising her will on the red-eye flight back to the West Coast after her mother's funeral, while I dozed in the seat beside her. *It can't be something you know in advance. If death does anything, it frees us— it opens that little door we slave our whole lives to keep closed, and lets us glimpse what freedom is. So let my death, when it comes, be a door that opens, not one you slam shut with hymns and tears and the same old frightened mewings. Let my death be a music you never heard before—let my death be that single moment you drop the protective crap and listen. And not in a church. Not that you couldn't do it in a church—you can do it anywhere. But the echoes are so thick in a church. Go out in the open air and throw me to the wind and listen. That's all I ask, is that you listen, for one moment in your life, to what my ashes say on the wind. It's such a simple thing, really. It's not so much to ask.*

—

The night passed somehow, to the clicking of the wheels. Sammy and I breakfasted in the dining car, a little giddily, on orange juice. It had been almost two days since we had eaten solid food by now; my body was doing what bodies do to adapt and I was feeling the strange peace that comes with hunger losing its urgency.

Sammy seemed to be showing no ill effects either. He had slept well and was still excited by being on a train. We spread maps again, reviewing our location in the grand scheme of things; and then he and I played cards for the rest of the bright, hot morning as we rolled on through lush New York countryside toward the city.

George Johnson met the train in Penn Station, something I should have been prepared for and yet wasn't. Sammy spotted him standing on the platform as we pulled in just after noon.

"Look, there's Grandpa!" he exclaimed, his nose pressed against the window.

I glanced out in the direction he was looking, but did not

spot Hannah's father right away. When I did recognize him at last, I was shocked by how much Johnson had aged since I had seen him last. In his early seventies now, Johnson had stopped dyeing his hair that lustrous black, and seemed to have lost quite a bit of weight. Standing there on the platform, gray and gaunt in loose-fitting casual slacks and some battered moccasin loafers, he looked a little like someone you might slip a dollar to as you went by.

Sammy, who saw his grandfather regularly on his own East Coast jaunts, waved through the window, but Johnson, looking weary and bereft, did not see him. I wondered if he was even expecting us to be on the train. It was his daughter, I was sure, whom he had come to meet.

The train eased to a stop. Sammy was up and down the aisle immediately; I followed more slowly. The two of them were embracing when I reached them, a long clinging hug, and Sammy was crying. Johnson was weeping too, which completely disarmed me. To my chagrin, I began to cry myself; and so, for some time, the three of us stood there on the noisy platform, while the busy crowd streamed on around us.

Johnson recovered first, releasing Sammy and straightening to blow his nose.

"Well, ah, welcome to New York, I suppose," he offered, with a weak smile. "I'm sorry it had to be like this."

He held out his hand and I took it. His grip was still firm— not the overwhelming clench of his potent middle age, but a handshake seasoned by grief and age and weakness like a wine, into warmth. In that moment I was still undone, and might simply have acceded to whatever machinery he proposed to remember his daughter by, so delicious did simple grief seem. LeeAnne was right, and Hannah was gone, and the world went on. I would make my home in the country of loss and forget all business.

"I'm sorry too," I said.

Sammy, who had been holding the scorched gift basket of Nebraskan bread and jam on his lap most of the way from Omaha, handed it to his grandfather now.

"Ah, what's this?" Johnson exclaimed obligingly, examining the heat-curdled plastic wrap.

"It's from Hannah," Sammy told him proudly.

"They found it in the van," I said. "Apparently she intended to mail it to you from the next town."

Johnson looked pained, but smiled for Sammy's sake. "Well, that's wonderful, Sammy. Thank you for bringing it to me."

But he handed the basket back to Sammy, I noticed. He bent and would have taken our suitcase, but I picked it up myself. The three of us walked up the stairs together.

"I've arranged for the body to be taken to McGreavy's Funeral Home on Long Island," Johnson told me, a little cautiously. "He will, um, hold it, until the judge arrives at his decision."

"Okay."

"Are you still—that is, are you still determined to...?"

I met his gaze, and was moved again by his watery, reddened eyes. The poor guy was hanging by a thread, as I was. But I answered firmly. "Yes. I am. I owe her that much, as a friend."

Johnson sighed.

"I don't know what I did wrong as a father...No, that's not

even entirely true—I know a great deal about what I did wrong. I drove her away, and I made her fight. I pressured her to be something she wasn't, and I never quite understood what it was that she *was*. It's too late to change any of that, and I have to live with it. But I'll do right by my daughter now, at least, Jeremiah. I guarantee you that. I'll see that she's given a proper farewell."

"I think you should read her will, at least. I think you should see how strongly she felt about this."

Johnson shrugged. "Of course." But the lines were drawn again. We walked in silence through the terminal to the baggage office, to confirm Johnson's arrangements, a painfully dry bit of business. I had a slip of paper, amounting to a claim check for the body of my best friend, which I surrendered to a man in shirtsleeves.

Afterward, we stepped back out into the bustle of the terminal and stood uncertainly for a moment near the shoeshine stand.

"Sam's room is ready, back at the house," Johnson said. "Same room he always stays in, it's already set up. But I'm afraid I had to give you Hannah's old room, Jeremiah, and it's not exactly—"

"We'll be staying at a hotel, of course."

"Nonsense."

We stood facing each other. Johnson was holding Sammy's hand, and I had the distinct sense that he was not going to let go. Sam himself had a look on his face that amounted to a plea for peace. I suppose my son saw more of Hannah in George Johnson than I ever did; and, at last, I shrugged my surrender.

"I've got the car in a garage up the street," Johnson said, mildly enough, not rubbing it in. "God, I hate driving into Manhattan, these hourly rates are murder."

"It's the same thing in downtown San Francisco."

"No, no," Johnson insisted cheerfully. "Manhattan is worse. It's the *worst.*"

"I suppose it is," I said resignedly. I was outgunned here, any way you looked at it.

---

Throughout the summer after Hannah's mother died, I could feel Hannah slipping away from me. There were obvious reasons for the distance. LeeAnne and I were "dating" again now, self-consciously going to movies and taking walks and having meals together, exchanging cautious good-night kisses at the ends of the outings like two people learning to walk again after broken legs. I was newly absorbed in a round of painting, post-Klee, had no patience for angels, and had stopped going up to Inverness. But it was more than that. Hannah was leaving *everyone* behind. On the construction site, she was peremptory and driven, and easily frustrated, as if the future of the new society of free and loving beings really rested on Jarmine's feeble drywalling skills or Bobby Van Knott's ability to swing a hammer stoned. Hannah had stopped sleeping with Albert by now, but she was pushing him hard, because he was the only one besides herself who could get anything done. Essentially the two of them were building the house alone, but I don't think either of them could have said anymore *why* they were building it. The clovers continued to die by natural and unnatural means, and all pretence of joy had gone out of the work of building. But it was Hannah's way, it had always been, to push, push, push, until a situation blew.

I did what I could to reach out to her, but I was handicapped by having opted—ignominiously, in Hannah's eyes—for picket-fence love and art, and Hannah treated me badly too. She clearly felt that I had let her down. It was the heart of our old pattern: I curved back toward the usual earth at critical moments, weighed down by human gravity, while Hannah was always looking for escape velocity.

—

That August, LeeAnne and I moved into an apartment together, on Tenth Avenue near Judah Street in San Francisco's Inner Sunset. I carried her across the threshold, a grand romantic flourish not without its irony (I had after all carried her across our previous threshold as well). But we were prepared to hope by then that practice makes perfect. Certainly I keenly felt the miraculousness of my second chance with LeeAnne, and would have carried her gladly up all three flights of stairs on a daily basis if it would have helped the cause of love.

The apartment, on the top floor of a funky old plaster building, was a bargain. It had two spacious rooms connected by battered French doors, beautiful bare wood floors, and great light. The whitewashed walls shuddered with the passing N-Judah trains. You could see the park two blocks away across the rooftops and in the late afternoon you could stand at the front room's bay window and watch the fog run in from the coast, right up Judah Street as if along the train tracks.

We had no furniture at first, but I had forgotten LeeAnne's gift for civilization-against-all-odds. She had two old silver candlesticks from her maternal grandmother, and she would bring them out for meals and burn tall candles that smelled gently of fruit. We ate Chinese take-out food by candlelight every night for our first two weeks in the place, drinking Tsing Tao beer out of the green bottles, exploring the subtle local variants of kung pao chicken and mu shu pork, and taping the inevitably auspicious pink fortune cookie slips to the refrigerator door: A NEW PHASE HAS BEGUN FOR YOU. YOUR PRESENT PLANS ARE GOING TO SUCCEED. LOVE CONQUERS ALL.

In bed—for quite some time a cheap foam rubber mattress on the floor, covered with a hundred-and-fifty-year-old quilt from another of LeeAnne's grandmothers—we laughed like children and made love like newlyweds and slept in the old familiar spoon position as if we'd been married for fifty years. LeeAnne's hair smelled of strawberry from the candles and I would wake sometimes in the night from a rich contented doze and breathe in that sweet scent. It smelled like home to me.

About a month after LeeAnne and I moved in together, Hannah fell off a scaffold at the Inverness house and hit her head so badly that the doctors said she might not survive. I got the call from a slightly hysterical Albert on a Thursday afternoon. At first I thought he was overreacting to a minor accident; but as the reality of the situation registered on me I was shocked by an electric jolt of terror at the thought of losing Hannah. I had been painfully conscious of our recent distance, seeing it as a phase, regrettable but natural enough under the circumstances. Trusting our mystical connection, believing there would always be time to meet again somewhere down the line, I had been inclined to let Hannah run out her furious construction phase while I enjoyed my second honeymoon with LeeAnne.

I drove to the hospital in a fury, prepared to battle anything that stood in my way. The looks on the faces of Albert, Bobby, and Jarmine in the waiting room, mournful and a little shifty, dodging responsibility, only made me madder. I stormed down the hall, shouldered past two doctors and a nurse to Hannah's bedside, and realized instantly that all the fury in the world would not give me another moment with Hannah. Her gray face was lifeless, beyond appeal, almost unrecognizable beneath a turban of white gauze, and her body seemed to have collapsed and lost its shape.

I stood helplessly by her bed and stared, my baffled rage churning slowly into panic, still feeling vaguely that it wasn't real, that it couldn't be real, that any instant she would wake, and wink.

"Hannah?" I said. "Hannah, can you hear me?"

"Sir, please...," the nurse said gently, easing me toward the door. "We're doing everything we can."

In the hallway, I found a chair and settled numbly into it, facing a blank wall, oblivious to the busy hospital traffic. It seemed too soon to grieve and too late to fight; what I really felt was loneliness, as sudden and keen as an unsheathed knife. For years, I had taken courage in Hannah's courage, and found faith in her faith; I counted on her laugh and her seasoned swagger, her joy in life and her wild, silly confidence. Seeing her face with the fire drained from it scared me more than anything ever had, and the thought of life without her scared me even more.

Hannah was unconscious for four days, a limp bit of flesh riddled with intravenous tubes and monitor wires, in a bed in intensive care. George Johnson flew out immediately and spent a lot of the time at the bedside, making a nuisance of himself with the doctors, and turning rosary beads over and over in his hand, a habit he had acquired while his wife was dying. His eyes said he blamed me, as he had always promised he would, and we were cautious with each other. Each day we sat on opposite sides of Hannah's bed and prayed our different prayers.

Albert, Bobby, and Jarmine came by every day, baffled, somber, and tentative. Bobby, in some low mushroom orbit of grief, believed he was conversing with Hannah's loosened spirit in the vast realm of the in-between, but he kept his reports to the minimum, in deference to Hannah's father. Jarmine spent most of her hospital time just trying to keep her bracelets from jangling. She believed vaguely that death was a good thing; at least it was so according to her understanding of Rajneesh. But Albert, who had made the faulty scaffold, was inconsolable. He had taken the loss of his intimacy with Hannah badly from the start, and had hung on bitterly, and now he was toying with deep, cruel, crazed notions of his own responsibility. It almost did him in.

All I could do was sit helplessly by the bed, day by day, listening to George Johnson click those awful beads. I had always more than half-believed Hannah's sense of her own mortality; I felt absurdly secure in her confidence that she would not die before her art had ripened. But the truth in her lifeless face was inescapable. I knew now that we had been fooling ourselves. Hannah could die, as anyone could die, with her music incomplete and our friendship in disarray, leaving all the things we'd believed we had years to perfect like a half-cooked soufflé, runny with old romance and vague dreams. I could hardly bear the thought of all the time we'd wasted.

LeeAnne stayed home, for the most part. I had been half-afraid she would make things difficult for me, would roll her eyes at Hannah's timing or otherwise begrudge me my vigil at the hospital. She was too noble and too proud to say a word, but I was leery of what she must be thinking. Our fragile, nascent domesticity had been trumped again. Yet LeeAnne was wiser than that, when it came down to it, and more loving. When I did manage to stagger home to shower and change clothes and collapse into our bed for an hour or two, she simply held me and talked about what I seemed to need to talk about, which was usually blood pressure and hyperalimentation and the likelihood of brain damage; and Lee-Anne's arms were the only place I found to cry during this period.

Before my inevitable return to the hospital, I would wander around our apartment, dazedly, feeling like a ghost amid the already precious familiarities of the place. Before Hannah's fall, LeeAnne and I had been gradually furnishing, filling in the odd rug here and the odd chair there, frequenting junk shops and garage sales for the joy of occasionally discovering a treasure. I had been working on a series of still lifes—domestic landscapes, as I thought of them—studies of our home as it took shape. But the paint had dried on my palette, which I had set aside the day the call from the hospital came; and dust had settled on my canvases. I would look at my sketches now and marvel at their incompleteness, at the fine line here that seemed perfectly true but needed other lines, at the patch of color there on a field of unshaped white: works in progress, merely, like our apartment. Or like my love for LeeAnne itself, I could not help but think: that delicate notion, nuanced and pencil-shaded, growing stroke by feather-stroke through a thousand daily touches into marriage. Or my love for Hannah, that watercolor study, far from finished in my own mind, of a friendship between two souls.

When I stayed too long at the hospital, LeeAnne would show up there herself, with a sandwich for me in a brown paper bag. While the IV bags dangled and dripped and the pump made its stolid, rhythmic click and whir, I would eat whatever my wife had made for me. The hands of the clock were meaningless to me by then, like semaphore signals or ancient hieroglyphics, and what I owed Hannah and what I owed LeeAnne, what I owed art and what I owed the world, all disappeared as those runic hands went round. *Give me another chance to show you what it meant to me,* I would silently beseech Hannah's lifeless face. *Give me another chance to try to get it right.*

From time to time her lids would flicker as the eyes beneath them moved, as if in dreaming. I took such movement eagerly for the hopeful sign it was. And so I sat by Hannah's bed and waited, while across from me George Johnson sat and prayed.

—

Hannah woke at about three in the morning, on the fifth day after her fall, and promptly started trying to tear the IV tubes out of her arms. I was the only one in the room at that point, and so was forced to wrestle with her. It was a terrifying experience at first, completely unnerving. Hannah was as frenzied as a netted wildcat, and her eyes were wild, eerily without a glimmer of recognition in them. She didn't say a word, only repeatedly tore at anything she could reach to get herself loose. Flailing and battering at my face and arms, she landed a couple punches that really rocked me, but in an odd way the pain only made me realize how desperately disoriented Hannah was, and how terrified. She had no idea where she was yet and all she wanted was to fight free.

It was all I could do to keep a single tube in her until several nurses showed up to help. They gave her some kind of shot to calm her down. I was so electrified with adrenaline by then that I could have used a sedative myself. As Hannah sank back toward unconsciousness, her eyes cleared for a moment, just long enough to meet mine with a gaze that was part accusation and part long-suffering and forebearance. *Forgive them, for they know not what they do.* She had blackened my eye and split my lip, but the blood tasted sweet to me. I was just so glad to see her awake.

The same thing happened the next time she woke up, and t he next. I took to wearing long-sleeved shirts to the hospital, as my arms were tracked and gouged from Hannah's finger-nails.

George Johnson took his rosary out into the hall during these episodes; he couldn't even bear to be in the room when his daughter was conscious. She started fighting the second she woke up and fought for as long as she was awake. I think her father took it personally. The doctors meanwhile were diag-nosing some kind of psychosis due to brain damage. But it was my sense that Hannah simply didn't want to be there yet, in the broad crudeness of daylight. There was a weird considera-tion in her eyes now when we wrestled, a kind of musing and assessment; she was testing out her forgotten powers, finding her way back to the world by fighting, because deep in her spirit that was what she knew how to do with the world. Unnerving as it was, I was glad to grapple with her, because it meant that she was alive.

One day after about a week of this, I woke from a brief doze to a gray dawn sky outside the window. The room was still, but I realized that Hannah was awake. I tensed, waiting for her to make her move. I had acquired a tremendous respect for Han-nah as an opponent by then. But she just lay still, watching me watch her, her deep blue-violet eyes impassive. And something in me thrilled: She was *back*. It was so simple, just like that, like waking from a dream.

It would be days before she said a word, and Hannah never did talk much about her experience. Not with me, anyway. Perhaps I had disqualified myself somehow, wrestling with her like that. Bobby Van Knott continued to suggest that Hannah had made the shaman's journey through the heavens and the hells in better style than I was prepared to credit, but Hannah herself supplied no details.

I was not all that interested, to tell you the truth. I didn't care a fig for the heavens and the hells, and I felt I had made enough of my own soul journeys at that bedside, weighing the feather of my heart against the immensity of loss. I was just glad to have Hannah back. Her silences were enough for me, and during her last week in the hospital we spent hours sitting in her room without a word, watching the light move across the city outside her window. From the thirteenth floor of the hospital, the view was extraordinary.

At first I kept trying to sketch her, out of sheer exuberance at seeing life in her face again, and my deepened sense of fleeting time. But Hannah broke my pencil on the second day, with a pointed grimace. I took it as a lesson, and a gift. After that we just sat quietly together, in a scorched sort of peace that needed nothing to complete it, and when we did talk, it was mostly about eating. Hannah had come back from the great beyond with a craving for Mexican food.

George Johnson went back to New York within two days of Hannah's resurfacing. In ordinary consciousness, the two of them had as little to share as they ever had. Johnson had apparently neglected the maintenance of his shiny black hair in the weeks he had spent on the West Coast, and the last time I saw him, bending over the hospital bed to kiss his daughter cautiously good-bye, the first ashen color was showing at the roots. It would be almost thirteen years before I saw him again, as I arrived on the train that carried Hannah's casket, and by then he would be entirely gray.

In the car on the way to George Johnson's house on Long Island, Sam sat in the front seat and talked baseball with his grandfather. Johnson had determined that Sammy needed distraction and was flourishing the sport like garlic at a vampire. He even had some scheme to get Sammy some time with the local Little League team. They needed a shortstop, according to Johnson, for some upcoming game; and he had already promised the coach his grandson could fill the gap.

It was not my sense that Sam *wanted* his mind taken off Hannah, but my son's grave indulgence of his grandfather moved me. I sat in the Lincoln's huge back seat without interfering, letting them work it out and marveling at the kid's aplomb. It was LeeAnne's doing, of course—certainly Sammy had not learned his social graces from Hannah or me. I felt surly and precarious, myself, on the verge of some kind of mayhem, and I had a fierce craving for a hamburger.

We got off the expressway at Jericho and headed north. Johnson lived in a woodsy suburb near Oyster Bay, close enough to the Sound to smell salt in the air. The big neocolonial house was set well back from the road, framed by oaks and sycamores across a grassy expanse. The Lincoln was the only car in the three-car garage and most of the house's downstairs rooms had the musty air of having settled into disuse. Johnson ushered me to the second-floor bedroom that had once been Hannah's, gave me towels, and pointed me to the shower. Then, though clearly tired himself, he hurried off to play catch with Sammy, as he had promised. I watched from the window as the two of them threw a ball back and forth in the backyard, trying to see whether I should go plead exhaustion for Sammy, to get him out of it. But my son was inscrutable, showing just enough genuine pleasure in their play to incline me to let them be.

The single bed Hannah had slept in as a teenager was crisply made, covered with a layer of quiet dust. On walls of slightly faded mauve were posters of John Lee Hooker and a young Eric Clapton. The bedside table's alarm clock was stopped near some ancient noon or midnight—it had probably not been wound in twenty years. Beside it, under the lamp, a copy of *Siddhartha* lay with its bookmark showing, as if she'd set it down expecting to come back to her reading later. And on the dresser, the only dusted spot in the room, was a picture of Hannah at fifteen or so, on some lawn somewhere, meeting the camera's eye in a New York Islanders sweatshirt and torn jeans, her face heartbreakingly bright and eager as a puppy's. She was holding her guitar by the neck, casual and cocksure. She'd scolded me once—about two months before she died—for picking up a guitar like that, but I suppose we both had learned a thing or two along the way.

## thirteen

## the view from tamalpais

Sometimes a grief like storm-wind sweeps away
All the words I found to bring you.
I shake helpless, silent as a corpse.
"Be happy," you say. "Now you are nothing."

Rumi

**George Johnson** had made meatloaf for dinner, in poignant anticipation of our arrival. Sammy informed him earnestly that we were fasting. Johnson blinked, then covered the pan with aluminum foil without a word, and put it in the refrigerator. If we weren't eating, he wouldn't eat either. If souls could laugh, I suppose Hannah was laughing somewhere at the three of us. To be frank, my mouth had watered at the sight of that meatloaf.

In lieu of dinner, Johnson poured himself a conspicuous glass of water I suspected he would spike with Scotch, before removing himself to his study with Hannah's will, like a seagull with a clam. We had continued to treat each other throughout the afternoon with an elaborate politeness, but we both were aware we would be doing battle the next morning, and it was a relief to have him gone.

After Johnson left, Sammy took a bath. Then he and I watched television for a while in the big, lonely den downstairs, nestled against each other on the couch, quiet and a little stupefied by the long day, before I took him up to his room and tucked him into bed.

Sammy had taken care, I noted, to put his keyboard on the bedside table, beside his baseball glove and the map of Nebraska.

"You know, you don't have to do all this baseball stuff, if you don't want to," I told him, as he settled under the blanket.

Sammy shrugged. "It's okay."

"Just so you know. I'll back you all the way."

"It's really okay, Dad."

"Okay." I kissed him good night, turned off the light, and went down the hall to brush my teeth, wishing LeeAnne were there. I had never felt my shortcomings as a parent more painfully.

As I came back from the bathroom, on my way to bed, I paused at the door of Sammy's bedroom and listened. Sure enough, in the darkness within, muffled slightly by the little tent the blanket made, I could hear the clicking of the keys.

———

We were scheduled to appear before the judge at ten the next morning. Sammy was left in the care of a neighbor, a kindly woman who had apparently been making George Johnson casseroles since his wife had died. Johnson and I left the Lincoln in a vast parking lot in Jericho and took the train into the city with the late commute crowd. Fortunately the car was nearly full; we found seats on opposite sides of the aisle and made the trip without having to exchange a word with each other. Johnson put on his reading glasses and reviewed a stack of papers from his briefcase, while I looked over Hannah's will in desultory fashion, moved as always by the urgent beauty of her handwriting and nearly overwhelmed by a sense of unreality. The will itself still seemed unambiguous enough to give me hope that even a judge who had been playing golf with Johnson for thirty years could read it only one way.

*And for God's sake, Mason, don't get all hung up on what to say or what to do or how to be, when the moment comes. You've been training for this thing your whole life. It's an empty canvas and I'm a brushstroke that surprises you. Think of it that way. I'll be ashes and you'll no doubt be all fucked up and sentimental, but try not to let that be the whole damn thing. We've seen each other ride the Big Ridiculous down to zero so many times by now, one more shouldn't be that big a deal. Despair is easy. Even grief is easy, when it comes to that. The real surprise is when love moves your hand.*

All around me, focused men in suits and ties read *The New York Times* and Tom Clancy novels. Certainly I was the only one on the train with paint on my pants. By now, I regretted the decision I had made in California to wear my working jeans, but my khakis wouldn't have been much better anyway, running with this crowd. I had turned down Johnson's offer—

gracious, under the circumstances—of a suit of his own for the occasion. The last thing I wanted was to plead Hannah's case in court while disguised as her father. I would render Caesar's unto Caesar, looking like hell, and leave the rest to God.

—

Not long after Hannah got out of the hospital, a forest fire broke out in the Inverness region and burned out of control for three long days. All access to our land was cut off, but we gathered from the evening news reports that our eighty acres were near the center of the action. Sure enough, when the roads were opened again, we drove north and found the house burned down to the foundation, and both hillsides scorched to naked black earth.

It was an unreal scene of total devastation. In every direction, as far as the eye could see, the terrain was blackened. The ground was still warm, and even smoking in places, as we walked around in grim silence, stepping tentatively on the unfamiliar surface, taking in the completeness of the destruction. Here and there the black skeleton of a manzanita shrub protruded from the burned dirt, but there was not a scrap of green remaining anywhere. We made our perfunctory searches, but one glance told the story. Mother Nature had accomplished what our clumsy intermittent efforts to save the species had been doing hit-or-miss, and wiped out the Kundalee Clover.

Of the house-in-progress, only the concrete foundation remained, deep in charred wreckage. What equipment we had left on the site was ruined, with nothing left but the heads of a few hammers and the blades of saws. Our stacks of plywood, boards, and drywall were gone.

Jarmine was weeping, the tears making trails down her slightly sooty cheeks, the jangle of her bracelets loud in the desolate silence of the place. She kept coughing, a dispirited hack; the air was still thick with smoke. Albert, with a stoic look, was collecting the hammer heads and blackened saw blades, perhaps with an eye toward salvage, perhaps just blindly. Bobby Van Knott had staggered off somewhere like a shell-shocked soldier to commune with the spirits of the destroyed vegetation. He had been running a sympathetic fever for days, and looked like hell.

Hannah and I crossed the dry channel of the seasonal creek and climbed the west hill to the ridge. We sat down on the blackened ground. From here, unburned forest could be seen across the valley, an incongruous swath of living color where a road and a stream and a change of wind had stopped the fire at last; but in between was only decimation, an eerie, feature-less no man's land broken by the black hulks of trees.

I scraped at the ground beside me. Two inches down, past cinders and ash, the dirt was brown again, with a slight baked quality. To my right, the faceted stump of a fern jutted stub-bornly. Unlikely as it seemed, I knew such remnants would be the first things showing green, after a touch of fog or a little rain. But I felt as desolate as the land itself.

Hannah picked up her own handful of the burned dirt and crushed it idly in her hand, watching the ash sift through her fingers. Below us, Albert and Jarmine had wandered back together and were embracing, comforting each other like the survivors in the last scene of some surreal apocalyptic movie. And all around us, everything smelled of smoke; the silence itself was heavy with smoke.

"This is what it felt like, waking up," Hannah said.

—

She had been quiet, keeping to her room, since she got out of the hospital, and after the fire she was quieter still. Everyone seemed a little afraid of her, including me. During her convalescence I would get across the Bay as often as I could to visit, perhaps twice a week, and every time I walked into the Durant Street house that hush would be on the place. Hannah's door would be closed, and everyone else would be tiptoeing around, a little bit adrift. There had never been a question of resuming work on the Inverness land. Albert was already talking about going back to school and Bobby Van Knott was talking about going to Oregon, or the Sierras. Jarmine's orange wardrobe was gradually diluted, at first by somber browns and then by greens, like a landscape after a fire. She was thinking of opening a metaphysical bookstore.

In the end, the Durant Street household broke quietly apart within a month. Everyone seemed secretly relieved by then, and they all went their separate ways without much fuss.

I helped Hannah move to her new place on a weekend in October. She'd found a cheap apartment above a Chinese restaurant on Irving Street, about three blocks from LeeAnne's and my place on Tenth Avenue. We hauled her few boxes of belongings up the narrow, dark stairs. The apartment had only two rooms, a kitchen and a bedroom, but Hannah's earthly possessions barely registered in the empty space.

As I brought one of the last boxes of books in, I found Hannah sitting on her guitar case. She'd taken out her old Martin and was strumming a few soft chords, wincing at how out-of-tune the thing was.

I must have looked ridiculously delighted, because she smiled at me ruefully. "If you make a big deal out of this, I swear I'll kick your ass."

I held up my hands in broad mock innocence, and went back out to get the last of her boxes out of the car. By the time I started up the stairs again, Hannah had the Martin tuned. I paused on the landing to listen as she began to play: a few finger exercises, some Blind Lemon Jefferson, and then, breathtakingly, Vivaldi.

I had to smile. George Johnson would no doubt have been secretly pleased—back from the grave, his daughter was practicing her scales, and playing dead people's music.

In the weeks and months that followed, Hannah played more and more often, branching out to reclaim most of her old repertoire, and reestablishing her calluses. We took to hanging out together while she practiced and had a sort of second honeymoon, artistically.

This was tricky, of course: LeeAnne had a natural, prudent, and enduring suspicion of my relationship with Hannah. But the brush with losing Hannah had fortified me in my determination to honor my bond with her. I loved LeeAnne, and as our marriage deepened I loved her more; but I loved Hannah too, with a love as deep and as real in its way, and I could not reconcile myself to letting go of the relationship because it did not fit into the simple categories. For lack of a better word, I called it a "friendship," but I treated it like orchids grown in a northern latitude, with hothouse tenderness. If Hannah and I had actually been having an affair, there was no way I could have pulled it off. But somewhere between the sexual tension and the guilt, the fear of losing LeeAnne and the fear of losing Hannah, was a narrow path of genuine friendship, requiring as much commitment and integrity as art itself, and I walked the fine line gratefully, teetering now one way, now the other, but managing to keep my balance.

A degree of ritual gave the uneasy arrangement a measure of stability. Twice a week, on Tuesdays and Thursdays, I would walk over to Hannah's after I'd finished my morning painting, and do watercolors at her kitchen table while she practiced her guitar. We would have lunch together, but not dinner; one beer in the afternoon, perhaps, but certainly not two; and I would come home before dark.

These days were precious. Hannah's music had a new, unhurried quality, a peacefulness and a vibrancy; while I was painting the Zen ox-herding cycle again, to her great amusement. We joked that the only difference from the barn loft in Utah was how much warmer it was now, and that we were not having sex. And indeed, having come full circle, unexpectedly, I was astonished at how much of what I had suspected as an apprentice had held up even through my foolishness and journeyman mistakes.

As the weeks went by, and settled into months, I watched Hannah continue to work and play, steady and serene. It seemed clear to me that we had finally come upon what we were meant to do. While Hannah ran her scales, and patiently fleshed out her repertoire, going over and over the simplest ground, I found discipline in the pattern of branches in her backyard's cypress, or the lines of a rickety fence—traces of wild freedom tempered into form. Everyone thought I had gone abstract, completely, but I was seeing more clearly and more immediately than ever. I was just seeing differently, with a calm, steady eye for the essential: seeing every line as if it had been drawn in the earth by a plow.

I tried to explain to LeeAnne the quality of Hannah's reinvigorated musical practice, its contagious new assurance and strength. But LeeAnne was sure I was just working up to sleeping with Hannah again.

"I should have *known,* of course. The past-life connection between the two of you is just way too strong."

"Sex is not the point," I insisted, painfully aware that my crediblity was thin. "Maybe in Pleistocene times, or the thirteenth century. Ten *years* ago, maybe. But not any more."

"Yeah, right," LeeAnne said. She wavered between believing we could weather another, inevitable fiasco, and insisting she would kill me. She and I had spent almost a year by then reclaiming our relationship like Dutch land from the sea after a breached dike, and LeeAnne was afraid all that work had been wasted. But I was sure that too much had changed since the last time the sea poured in. It was a question of self-knowledge. In the shakeout of everyday life, Hannah and I had discovered all the ways we were suited and not suited to each other; we knew each other's faults and quirks and weaknesses too well by now to fool ourselves. The two of us often laughed, indeed, that we would have hated each other in a situation where the dishes and laundry had to be done regularly. It was, in its way, a truth as dependable as the truths of art.

Hannah had begun to play in some local clubs by now, and LeeAnne and I would go to listen to her sometimes on a Friday night, taking a table near the back to keep from making Hannah nervous. Through the smoke and the noise, it always seemed impossible that Hannah would even be heard. She would walk quietly out to her stool and tune her guitar amid the hubbub, as she had tuned it by the fireplace at Burton's grandfather's house the first night I saw her, and, watching her, I was always afraid for her. Hannah seemed too delicate to dent the din.

But always, just when I thought it most impossible, she would finger her guitar and slip out boldly into song. Her voice would soar free. And I would sit stunned and awed all over again, as if for the first time. Hannah's latest songs were stronger than ever, sweet and warm and seasoned, a haunting blend of country folk and blues, with simple, insistent melodic lines. She sang one called "The Flame of Love" that I always half-suspected was addressed to me.

*I'll help you with the seeds that you are sowing—*
*I'll prop the fences up when the wind blows through.*

*But in the end there's no way out of knowing*
*That fire does the work we cannot do.*

The conversations in the room would slowly fade; by the second or third song, Hannah always had the crowd's attention. In Utah we had taken the miracle of her music in stride, and assumed the world must arrange itself around such magic when the moment came; but I understood now how fragile the miracle was, and how easily lost. What I loved most in Hannah was that she had found her way back, somehow, to what I had thought must be lost forever. So I would watch and listen through the smoke, just one of the rapt and silenced crowd now, holding LeeAnne's hand, as Hannah played.

One day about three years after her accident, Hannah and I drove up Mount Tamalpais with a picnic lunch on a Tuesday afternoon. The outing was a bit of a stretch, according to the strict conditions of the triangular truce with LeeAnne, but years of sexual uneventfulness had created some leeway by then.

We spent the afternoon sunning on a stone ledge of the wonderful WPA-built amphitheater carved into the hillside three-quarters of the way up the mountain. No one else was around. The beer was cold, the Indian summer sun was warm, and the air was clear as only the Bay Area's air can be, after weeks of fog. San Francisco and the East Bay showed crisply across a dreamlike gulf of blue beyond the treetops. The amphitheater itself slumbered in its timeless granite, the curving ledges falling away below us to a distant little wooden stage. I'd been here once with LeeAnne for a staging of *Macbeth* beneath the stars, but today the place was emptied of tragedy and comedy alike. While we sat there, three deer wandered out of the trees stage left, wary at first, then settling in to graze at the base of the platform, while the squirrels and bolder sparrows made pilgrimages to our feet to scrounge for crumbs.

Hannah had brought her guitar, but she left it in its case; I'd brought my sketchpads and watercolors, but the lazy sun was rich enough that day to make every palette mix seem poor, and I spent most of the afternoon simply luxuriating in the light, and trying to keep my beer in the shade. We'd both been working hard for months, in any case, and it was one of those days when life seems to lift you briefly above the fray to offer the clearest of views.

As the sun moved toward the edge of the mountain behind us, the shadows crept upward and the light over the Bay grew richer with rose and gold. Hannah tossed the last scrap of sandwich to a squirrel and settled against the stone behind her. I rummaged in the cooler for the last beer. I opened it up and offered a swig to Hannah, who drank deeply and handed it back. I raised the bottle to my own lips.

"I've decided to move back to the East Coast," Hannah said.

I laughed, assuming she was kidding.

"No, I'm serious," she insisted. I sat up. "I've been thinking about it ever since my mother died—realizing how little I tried to get to know her. My father's not getting any younger himself. If we're ever going to understand each other, now's the time to try."

"But you're just getting your act together here," I protested, aware that I was not taking it well.

"That's why now is exactly the time to do it. I'm finally working from strength, I've got a place to stand. I couldn't go back before, because I was going back with nothing. Now I think I've got the strength to look things in the face."

" 'Things' being your father?"

"Among others, yes. But not just him."

"He's just going to think you're dragging back there with your tail between your legs, you know. You feel like you're coming from strength, but he's going to see it as weakness."

"You're making my case. All I really want is for us to see each other clearly."

"Maybe you're just feeling guilty that his fifty thousand bucks disappeared with the Kundalee Clover. You want to make amends."

Hannah shrugged. "I don't think it's that."

"Besides," I persisted, growing frankly desperate, "you always told me how much you hated the winters in New York."

Hannah laughed. "Look, Mason, it's just a sense I have, that it's where the next round of work is to be done. I'm not sure myself exactly what that means. Sometimes all you can see is one step ahead. But I see this one pretty clear. It's time to move on." She smiled. "I would think you'd be overjoyed about this. You always told me California was unreal."

"That was when you were leaving *Utah*. I never meant to imply New York was realer."

Hannah laughed again, and I knew then, from the lightness and tender indulgence of it, that she was serious.

"This is so *like* you," I exclaimed. "This is so goddamned perfectly completely *characteristic*. Just when things start to get good, just when you're on the verge of doing some good work right where you are…Do you know what I think? I think you just can't stand happiness. You can't stand a good normal dose of simple peace. It seems too petty to you. Only trouble is grand enough."

"I think that what you're calling happiness is just this little thing that happens in the sun on a mountain on a perfect day a couple times a year for about an hour and a half. But you can't stay on the mountain all the time, Mason."

I was silent, no doubt sullenly so.

"I don't want to fight about *this*," Hannah said, more gently. "Not with you. I want you to understand. I have to go."

Below us, the deer had left; the whole amphitheater was gray with shadow now, and the air was cooling. The hillside poppies were closing up for the night. Across the Bay, the sunlight glinted off windows in the Berkeley hills.

Hannah reached over and took my hand. "Look, Mason, it's just something that I feel like I've got to do. Call it karma. Or just plain timing, I suppose."

"Karma is for Hindus and Buddhists," I snapped. "Timing is for carburetors. This is good old Judeo-Christian stupidity."

She smiled indulgently. We sat for a moment without speaking. Then Hannah reached for her guitar, tuned up, and began to play "White Empty Canvas"—as a sop to me, I was sure. By then Hannah had long since come to think she'd outgrown the first song I ever heard her play. But she played it out of kindness, as a good-bye gift to my simple ear.

*So love the flames the way you love the growing,*
*And love the ashes like the morning dew:*
*All things arise and all things must be going,*
*And fire does the work we cannot do.*

Hannah left for the East Coast three days later, despite my continuing efforts to dissuade her. I found myself in the strange position of defending Californian civilization as a work-in-progress, but Hannah was adamant. Her reasoning continued to be vague; she missed the turning of the autumn leaves. She even missed the snow. But in the end it was intuition—Hannah simply felt the need to go home.

All her belongings still fit in the back of her old Datsun hatchback—Hannah had always prided herself that she could hit the road at a moment's notice. She'd decided to take the southern route across the United States, down the east side of the Sierras, and out of California through Death Valley. She asked me to ride with her as far as Las Vegas and I agreed, which caused a bit of a fuss at home. I told LeeAnne that I owed Hannah that much at least; and LeeAnne, who clearly believed the trip to be a setup for catastrophe, rolled her eyes and shrugged, which I took for her consent. We had moved out of the Tenth Avenue apartment the year before to a place on Thirty-Eighth, a wonderful in-law apartment with a homely little backyard we had converted to a garden, and a view of the ocean. There had been no sexual ripples between Hannah and me for years, and it seemed to me we were all on solid ground. I told LeeAnne it was like taking my aunt someplace. It was like a slightly extended Tuesday afternoon.

"Yeah, right," she said dryly, but she let me go.

Hannah and I left late in the day, a week before Halloween, in the face of warnings of an early storm that Hannah said we could beat to the mountains. We ran ahead of the weather front most of the way, passing through South Lake Tahoe on dry streets at around midnight and turning south on 395 as the first snowflakes began to fall. Most of the little roadside motels were closed up for the night by then, and we drove another two hours south before we found a place that would take us in. The sleepy guy at the desk gave us a room with a queen-size bed. Rather than wake him up again to ask for singles, Hannah and I climbed chastely in from opposite sides, relying on our spiritual maturity and well-established friendship to keep us warm and separate through the night.

For one long moment, it even seemed possible. Hannah said good-night and rolled over with her back to me, quite properly. We lay quietly in the darkness with the sheet still cool between us. But I was aware of my pounding heart, and the closeness of her; and at last I reached out and my hand found her hip, and I felt the warm bend where her leg met her body. An ache rose up in me like a flame and I knew then that it had been too much to ask of my simple flesh.

Hannah stiffened, cautiously, unencouraging; then, as I did not withdraw my hand, she rolled over to face me. In the filtered light of the neon motel sign through the curtain, I could just make out her features, and the somber depths of her eyes. She gave me a long, searching look, then raised her own fingertips, tentatively, to my cheek. I shivered at her touch, and turned my face into her hand.

"Ah, Jeremiah," Hannah breathed, almost sadly.

"I'm sorry," I whispered, whether to her or to LeeAnne or to myself, I didn't know. There was such a fierce, sweet longing in me. I touched her hand alongside my face, and kissed her fingers, gently, breathing in the scent of her skin, feeling my desire opening out like a long exquisite fall. Hannah's fingers tightened along my cheek, her touch firming into a caress, tilting my head toward her. My hand slid up the lush curve of her hip again, beneath her T-shirt to the warm hollow at the small of her back, and she arched toward me, her knee slipping between my legs. Our lips met and the years meant nothing and I knew that I was lost, and willingly, in that moment. I loved her so, and I had so missed the sweetness of her kiss.

The next morning I woke ashamed and heavy with the certainty that I had ruined all three of our lives. But Hannah was sober, perhaps even slightly amused, and gentle with us both, inclined to call it one for the road and take a mulligan. She knew as well as I did what LeeAnne meant to me; and she knew, even more clearly than I, that our lovemaking the night before, so poignant and lovely and far away from our real lives, had been a good-bye.

We drove on south, through serious snow now, the only car on the road for the most part. There were several touch-and-go points through the high passes but at last we descended into the finality of the desert country and headed east through the Panamint Range to Death Valley. On a blanket in the salt flat by Badwater, at the lowest point in the continental United States, we sat for meditation and I sketched her face, one last time, in the crisp dry air, with only the ravens for company.

At the state line, Hannah stopped the car and did a head-stand beneath the big green sign that said "Leaving California." I took a photograph, and to this day I still turn that picture over once in a while to look at Hannah's face right-side up, trying to understand what it all meant to her.

"Well, it's all yours," she told me that day, when she was upright again and standing on the Nevada side of the line. "Ironic, isn't it? That you should be the one to stay?"

"I've always been the one to stay," I said.

She smiled. "I suppose you have."

We drove on to Las Vegas, where Hannah kissed me good-bye and put me on a bus back to LeeAnne. We rode off in our opposite directions down the neon-lighted strip, and that was the last I saw of her for quite a while, though she wrote frequently enough, and always sent tapes of her latest music. Settling in on the south shore of Connecticut, across the Sound from her childhood home—close enough to make the appropriate efforts but far enough away to recover in between—Hannah wrote that she still found her father impossible. They hardly ever saw each other, and still mostly fought when they did, but she said she was learning to see her love for him through all the smoke of battle.

LeeAnne took one look at my conscience-stricken face

when I got back to San Francisco and went out into the back-yard with a gasoline can. She doused the garden liberally and threw a match, and the poppies and snapdragons and silvery sage went up in gorgeous flames. I remember standing in the back door watching it burn and thinking it was good. The Catholic theologians have always said that the difference between the fires of purgatory and the fires of hell is that the souls in purgatory suffer their penance willingly.

When the flames had died down into the scorched black dirt, I turned and went back into the house. LeeAnne had retreated into the bedroom and the door was closed. I knocked once, but she just said, wearily, "Go away, Jerry. We'll talk tomorrow."

I walked back into the living room and sat down on the couch. My clothes smelled of smoke. The sun was setting beyond our back window, and I sat there for a long time, watching all the precious, familiar furniture of the life we'd made together sink into shadow as the room got dark. Then I made the couch up and tried to get some sleep. I had done what I had done; in my heart, I wouldn't have changed it even if I could. There was nothing ahead of me now, though, but the long road back. I could still see that garden burning in my mind's eye, but LeeAnne had promised we would talk.

Hannah was playing in some New York clubs within weeks of her arrival on the East Coast, and looking for a bass player and a drummer, to form a band. All through that winter and spring, the news from her was mostly music, and the occasional spat with her father. It was not until the next June, indeed, long after LeeAnne had forgiven me for my indiscretions on the farewell jaunt down 395, that Hannah got around to telling me—about a month before Sammy was due—that we had conceived a son.

—

Judge Marquess Norman received us in his chambers. Some part of me had craved the glamour of defeat in open court, the noble speech in the hopeless cause before the rapt, uncomprehending throng. But in the end the matter was settled between reasonable men in a walnut-paneled room full of books, and what nobility I could muster was largely irrelevant.

Judge Norman, a pleasantly corpulent man of fifty-five or so, with bushy eyebrows gone mostly gray, sat in shirtsleeves behind an expanse of well-kept desk. He greeted us somberly, expressing his condolences to George Johnson and his hope that we could sort things out without adding to his pain at the loss of his daughter.

"It is my understanding that the question is of the disposal of the remains?"

"That's correct, Your Honor," Johnson said. "As you'll note in my brief, it is my position that, in the absence of an unambiguous statement to the contrary, the question of disposal should revert to the next of kin."

"Hmm," Norman said, and raised one wild eyebrow at me. "Mr. Mason?"

"Your Honor, Hannah left a will specifically stating her wishes in this matter. With all due respect to Mr. Johnson's loss, I am simply trying to see that her wishes are carried out."

"Um-hmm," the judge said. "And do you have a copy of that document?"

"I have the original, sir." I handed him the handwritten pages, uncomfortably aware of the sketches on the backs of several of them. Like any pages torn more or less at random from a sketchbook, the studies were a mixed bag; but the nudes struck me as prominent, all questions of quality aside.

Norman put his reading glasses on and settled in to review the will. It took him fifteen minutes to read the whole thing, during which time I became aware of the sensuous deep *tock* of a big brass ship's chronometer on the wall behind his desk. George Johnson sat in the chair beside me, his legs crossed, a length of gray silk sock sagging slightly on his ankle. We did not look at each other.

"Ah, well—" Judge Norman said at last, settling back in his lush leather chair, "It strikes me that this document is more poetic than specific."

I heard George Johnson's slight exhalation beside me; a sigh of relief.

"The language is rich," I conceded. "Perhaps a little over-rich, at times. But surely the essence is clear."

"The text is moving," Norman said. "It is highly moving. But I am inclined to see 'the embrace of the fire of mortality' as metaphorical, not legally significant."

He never banged a gavel, but that was that. There were handshakes all around. Norman handed the will back to me without ceremony and George Johnson and he promised to see each other soon for lunch. Johnson and I walked out together without a word. Part of my mind was doing an outraged dance of righteousness, racing ahead to take the case to the Supreme Court, to fight it out to the bitter end. But I had seen my ridiculousness in that office, sitting among the sets of law books, listening to the old clock tick and contemplating George Johnson's sad, exquisite sock, and the patch of aged leg above it. LeeAnne had been right, as always. It had never been a battle I was meant to win.

## fourteen

## te deum laudamus

And kingdoms

        naked in the

                trembling heart—

    Te Deum laudamus

              O Thou Hand of Fire

—Hart Crane, "Ave Maria"

*The funeral was held* the following morning—
George Johnson had been confident enough of a victory to
schedule it in advance. He had insisted on a small, private ceremony, and less than two dozen old friends of the family
attended. Several television stations had contacted Johnson by
now, and a number of reporters, but they had all been put off.
There were even a couple tabloid camera crews milling outside the church where the funeral Mass was held. The deaths
of Hannah and her band were resonating in the music world
with that touch of Buddy Holly glamour I believe she had

always hoped for. Apparently sales of her CD were way up, and you couldn't turn the radio on without hearing "A Walk in the Blinding Light." Strangers kept leaving flowers in piles at the foot of the driveway of the Oyster Bay house. But to look around the church that day, you'd have thought Hannah had outlived most of her cronies and died in her bed at eighty-five, with a rosary in her hand, so tiny and aged and Catholic was the crowd.

Sammy and I sat and stood and knelt beside George Johnson during the Mass. I felt weirdly detached throughout the proceedings, as if I'd stumbled into a stranger's funeral. It all had so heartbreakingly little to do with Hannah. I was wearing one of Johnson's sleek dark suits, which hung on me like a sack, and Sammy wore the suit LeeAnne had packed for him, and we both looked awkward and out of place.

Johnson, perhaps from misguided conscience, had prevailed upon me at the last moment to deliver a eulogy, as he had prevailed upon Hannah to play at her mother's funeral. I confess that I considered just walking up to the lectern and cranking up a boom box tape of some of Hannah's rowdier compositions, a futile exercise in guerrilla theater that I knew would have delighted her. But in the end, we all do what we can. I spoke briefly and from the heart, as if Sammy were the only one in the church. Hannah's music spoke for itself, after all, and those with ears to hear would find their way to it, but someone had to simply say this woman lived, and saw, and sang. To say that she was beautiful, and that she celebrated beauty. To say that she loved, and was loved, and that she would not be forgotten.

"I never wanted to be standing here," I told that little crowd of aged strangers, in conclusion. "It never seemed to me that what Hannah meant to me could possibly be said. But love is what is left when the dust all settles, and in the end it is our complications that do not matter..."

The cool little church was appropriately hushed; a few of the matrons were dabbing at their eyes. I wished again, briefly, that I had brought the boom box. I was thinking of a poem Hannah had shown me once, not long after she got out of the hospital after her coma. It was one of the few glimpses she had ever given me of what the experience had meant to her.

> I was among great souls,
> as if amid a flame,
> and all the things of earthly life
> were lost in that great brightness.
> I might have been afraid
> if fear had had a place
> to move in me at all.
> But there was no place for fear.

I took a breath. "The truth is that Hannah would have been laughing at this speech, and at all this solemnity. She would have said we are missing the point—or hiding from it, maybe. She had embraced her own death long ago, and made her peace with it. I think that is what set her free somehow, in the end—not to be grim, and to despair, but to dance, and to make her life a song of joy. Hannah taught me to trust that joy, as she taught me to trust love itself. I know that I will never be done being grateful to her. It's so inadequate, it hurts me even to say it . . . but God, I am going to miss her."

There was nothing else to say. There had never been anything to say in the first place that amounted to a thing. I stepped away from the lectern, feeling like shit, and made my way back to my seat. George Johnson was blowing his nose; and the matrons seemed content, which baffled me. Sammy was sitting solemn and upright in the pew. I took my place beside him, reached for his hand, and squeezed it as the organist cranked into something lugubrious and that dear old Catholic crowd mustered their voices for the hymn.

In the graveyard, in heavy August sunlight, more prayers were said, before Hannah's Nebraskan casket was lowered into a grave beside her mother's. I still had the key to that casket, entrusted to me in the Omaha train station by Harmon Tulliver, but it didn't seem to matter now. There would be no moving of the stone, no resurrection into ashes, and no ashes on the wind. I'd done my sad little best for Hannah, and made my little failure. Ahead was only a grief I could feel in myself like firewood stacked in a hearth—unlit, deferred for the moment as we went through these motions according to the world's cold script, but waiting, quietly, for its moment, with a promise of warm companionship through the winter's night to come.

Sammy was weeping quietly and I put my arm around him. A seminarian read from John of the Cross—

*If, then, I am no longer*
*Seen or found on the common,*
*You will say that I am lost;*
*That, stricken by love,*
*I lost myself, and was found—*

and the small crowd began to disperse. And still my hand kept creeping to my pocket, to finger that useless key, until at last Sammy and I and two guys with shovels were alone by the grave and I tossed it into the hole. The key clinked dully on the coffin's lid and lay still; I watched it disappear beneath the first shovelsful of dirt, then walked away with Sammy, while the men went on with their work.

Back at the house, Johnson's neighbor had laid out a touching buffet, and the mourners tucked in quietly. Some guitar music was playing in the background—I recognized the Vivaldi sonata Hannah had so labored over the winter her mother was dying. George Johnson must have edited the tape, transferring it selectively to an endless loop, because the version of "Friend of the Devil" I remembered following the sonata never came. There was just the faintest little *bloop* at the critical moment, like a swallowed hiccup, and then the exquisite Vivaldi again, over and over, as if it were the only music Hannah had ever played.

As I stood near one of the speakers, picturing Hannah's fingers on the strings, George Johnson approached me.

"Would you join me for a moment in my study?"

"Of course."

We slipped away through the crowded rooms; Johnson shut

his study's door with frank relief. It was the first time I had been in the room and the first thing I noticed was the portrait of Hannah on the wall behind the desk.

My arms prickled with gooseflesh. The work had held up well, all things considered. In the timeless painted moment, Hannah still sat by the big loft window on the rickety stool, absorbed and free, playing to the lavender mountains across the valley, for all the world as if there would never be anything else to do or anywhere else to go. *Girl with a guitar, north light.* In the bottom right-hand corner, in purple, was the angular "mason" I had used to sign things with, some twenty years ago.

"I bought you early," Johnson said, noticing my glance.

"I gave it to you, as I recall."

He smiled. "No. You only tried to give it to me. In the end, you took the check."

It was all coming back to me now. "I don't think Hannah ever forgave me for that."

"And I don't think I can ever be done being grateful. I've taken a lot of joy in that painting over the years. It was the side of her she never let me see."

I nodded absently. Hannah on that stool, by that window, brought it all back, indeed—the warm beauty of that cold time, the light, and the joy in light. The world abandoned for a song. But Johnson was right: I had cashed the check.

I turned away. The study had a warm, lived-in feel, unlike the rest of the house, as if it were the only place George Johnson still felt at home. Books on the shelves had the look of being recently handled, the photographs all were dusted, and the desk was an endearing mess.

By the window, two comfortable leather chairs had been placed on either side of a small table. The truck-stop gift basket Hannah had bought the day she died had been filled with flowers for a centerpiece, while the bread from it had been sliced and neatly laid out on a silver tray. The miniature jars of Nebraskan jam had been opened. A bottle of wine, also opened, stood between two wineglasses.

"I thought we might break our fast," George Johnson said.

"Of course," I said, hoping Sammy would forgive me. But there was no question of saying no. We moved together to the little table and busied ourselves briefly with the bread. Surprisingly, after all it had been through, it was quite good. The crust, twice-baked and flecked with melted plastic, was inedible as stone, but we tore the still-fresh inner bread away from it like children and ate it in little self-conscious bites. I even spread a bit of blackberry jam on mine. In the heightened moment, the sensuous purple of the jam seemed rich as oil paint beneath a palette knife. It seemed forever, suddenly, since I had stood before a canvas.

Johnson poured the wine and handed me a glass. "To Hannah?"

"To Hannah." I touched his glass and we drank. The wine was extraordinary, a lush burgundy with just a touch of smoke at the edge, that disappeared on the tongue.

"I'd been saving this for her wedding," Johnson said shyly. "Ridiculous, I know. But it's a marvelous vintage."

He was so afraid I'd mock him, it almost broke my heart. "It's delicious."

"Not that Hannah would have cared, of course, one way or

another. But it's the best, you see. I wanted her to have the best."

His voice broke slightly. We were silent a moment, looking at the bread on the plates.

"I wonder that she even thought to buy this for me," Johnson said at last. "The bread, I mean—it was just *like* her, wasn't it? One last bafflement. What was in her mind? Was it a *joke?*"

"It might have had a touch of tricky humor in it," I conceded. "A little play on the heartland kitsch. But a gift is a gift. She loved you, and was thinking about you."

He made a little sound of disbelief, his eyes fixed on his plate.

"It's true," I insisted. "She always said so. You're the main reason she came back east. She wanted to get her relationship with you right."

He glanced up, almost shyly. "No."

"Yes."

"But all we did was fight."

I smiled. "I know. She told me. Ad nauseam. And every time she did, all I could think was that I wished she'd stayed in California and fought with *me.*"

He took it in for a moment, then said, tentatively, "You're just telling me this to make me feel better."

"Not really. If you didn't understand she loved you, there's no help for you. I'm telling you because it's the truth."

Johnson resisted for a moment more, then shook his head and smiled. "Well, I'll be damned."

We sat down then and ate the bread in earnest, like the hungry men we were. The wine was already going to my head, but

I finished off a second glass. Then I excused myself and staggered out in search of Sammy. I had the last pieces of the bread with me on a china plate and was prepared to insist, but my son was way ahead of me, as he so often was. I found him in the kitchen, listening to the endless Vivaldi, perfectly content with a bowl of Frosted Flakes.

Later that afternoon, after the other mourners had gone and George Johnson had retired to his room for a nap, Sammy and I went down the road to find the spot in the woods where Hannah had wanted her ashes scattered.

I'd been here once before. Hannah had led me to the little clearing the day after her mother's funeral. The woods had been barren then, bleak and leafless and patchy with snow. We had smoked a cigarette or two, in perfunctory ritual, listening for the sparrow Hannah insisted sang the first five notes of "Summertime Blues." But there was nothing singing in those woods that day, not even Hannah herself, and at last we had fled for warmth, with a sense of vague defeat.

Today, the summer lushness was disorienting; it took Sammy and me almost an hour of wandering to come upon the place again. But there was no mistaking it once you came upon it, even in its luxuriant disguise of green. Two fallen trees made a right angle at the clearing's northern edge, with a view of the Sound; a creek ran along the south side, and the arc of glacial boulders defining the west edge gave a Stonehenge-like air to the spot. Hannah had insisted it was an old Indian site, and said she had found arrowheads here. A new generation had discovered the sanctuary and the ground was littered with beer cans, cigarette butts, and the occasional condom.

We sat down on the old fallen log where Hannah had sat as a teenager to practice the songs she didn't want to play at home. Her weathered initials were still visible in the wood. Sammy immediately wanted to carve his own initials beside hers; he took out his pocketknife and set to work. I sat beside him, empty-handed but strangely content, listening for the sparrow and watching Sammy work. I loved that look of quiet absorption on my son's face.

"You're going to have to take him anyway, eventually," Hannah had told me by telephone, just before I flew out to the East Coast for Sammy's birth. She'd had it all worked out in her mind; she was very clear. She had been determined to have the child—it was why she had waited until it was nearly a fait accompli to tell me about it—but she was just as determined that she couldn't keep him. She was alone and just starting out on a career in music that was going to take up all her time for the next ten years; while I was well-established in the practice of my art and was in a solid relationship with LeeAnne. That taking on Sammy might destroy both my feeble art and my relationship with LeeAnne was a point Hannah never chose to worry about. I could offer our son a decent home; she could not. The hell of it was that she was right, as far as that went, even without crediting her bizarre certainty that she would be dead before the kid was out of grade school. But of course it was not as easy as that.

The night before I left for the East Coast, LeeAnne and I had gone out into the backyard to watch the sunset and talk things over.

"Hannah wants me to take the kid," I said. "Wants *us* to take it, I mean—you and me."

LeeAnne was silent for a long moment. In the twilight, the fountain of our little birdbath gurgled. The garden around us was rich with poppies, blue columbine, milkwort, and flowering purple lavender; I'd turned the scorched black dirt under and replanted the previous spring and, if anything, the vegetation had come back lusher than ever since LeeAnne had burned it the year before.

"Well, that's damned nice of her," LeeAnne said at last. "And easy for her to say, of course."

I nodded unhappily, granting her the point. We were silent again. To the west, over the rooftops, the setting sun through the bank of offshore fog was a strange, cool orange. I had been half-hoping LeeAnne would simply throw a fit and let me off the hook. But the hook wasn't going anywhere, and at last I said, "LeeAnne, I love you. If you don't want to raise the kid with me, if this is going to wreck us, we'll put it up for adoption. I'm no damn hero, and I couldn't do this without you."

"It's a helluva time to finally realize *that*." LeeAnne shook her head wearily. "Look, Jerry, if I were going to leave you over this, I would have left you last year. Maybe I'm an idiot not to. I'm not going to pretend I'm thrilled with the situation. But what's done is done. We've got years to figure out what it all means, and to try to make it into something we can live with. But that poor kid is going to need its parents from the start.

Am I happy? No. Will I be a good mother to your little love child? Yes. And as for the rest of it, as for us, and for the marriage, we'll have to see. We'll just have to see if I can ever look at you again without wanting to spit."

She turned then and went into the house, leaving me in the cool settling dark, feeling shabby and ashamed. I was painfully aware that she had been more merciful than I had deserved and that she had not, necessarily, been merciful for my sake. LeeAnne had even refrained, at that critical moment, from belaboring the obvious: that I had fled from having a child with her.

I had flown out to the East Coast the next morning. When Hannah's labor came, I had stayed close, at her insistence, and held her hand through the long sweaty hours, while her father had kept his rosary vigil in the hall. The labor went on, and on, turned nightmarish, and then unreal, and still went on, through the night and the next day. The doctors kept shaking their heads at how narrow her hips were; Hannah herself had often said that she was never meant to breed.

In the end, after almost thirty-six hours, they nearly lost both of them, mother and child, and had to give Hannah an epidural and do an emergency C-section. She was so weak by then she couldn't even hold the child and so the nurse handed the baby boy to me. There was no one else to hand it to. It was the simple truth. I met Hannah's knowing, exhausted gaze across the bloody child in my arms, and smiled, a little sadly.

*Maybe you'll even hate me for a while,* she had written not long after that, in one last postscript to her will that left all her worldly goods to a trust for Sammy. *Maybe all good gardeners can't help but hate the storm. But in the end, you'll make it right. Root and stem, leaf and branch—you love the plant, dear Mason, you live for growth and all that good green healthy activity. It's a lovely thing. But somebody's got to flower once in a while. Somebody's got to burst into gaudy color for a moment and then disappear, a squandered beauty, for the seed to set.*

*Or maybe I'm not so pretty as all that—call me a pine tree, then, waiting for years for the forest to burn. All you can see is the scorched ground afterward, and the black skeletons of the trees. But I know it took the fire to make the cones surrender the seeds—I know the tree was born to await that flame, that it needed the fire to complete the cycle. Think of it that way if it helps. Think of it any damn way you want, my friend and my love. If you're reading this at all, I'm probably out of here.*

Sammy cocked his head suddenly. "There it is."

"What?"

"The sparrow. . . . Listen—"

We listened, but I couldn't pick anything particularly bluesy out of the hubbub of summer birds. My ear, for all my love of music, is not so very good. But I knew Sammy could hear it fine.

The next evening, our last on Long Island, George Johnson pulled his strings with the local Little League, as he had promised, and Sammy played the last three innings of a game at shortstop for the Meyers' Texaco Pelicans. While Johnson and I sat in the stands, rooting embarrassingly and nursing watery Diet Cokes, Sammy handled two ground balls and a pop-up without incident. He grounded out to third base his first time at bat, respectably enough, and I breathed a little easier. But in the bottom of the last inning, he came to bat for the second time with two outs and the bases loaded, and his team two runs behind.

The big banks of lights had come on by then, and the moths flitted around them. The outfield grass glowed emerald green. Down the right field line, a group of teenagers lounged, smoking cigarettes; and the bleachers were crowded with hopeful parents. The smell of hot dogs was on the air. It was twilight in America and my kid was up with the game on the line.

*Let him single to right,* I prayed. *That's all—an off-field, two-run single to tie the game. He doesn't have to hit it over the fence, to have a decent life.* It seemed to me somehow, in the ridiculous moment, that Sammy could be saved from a life of art—and even, magically, from heartache—by one good, clean base hit. But he lined out to shortstop on the second pitch.

"Ah, well," George Johnson said, as we drove home, "You'll get 'em next time, Sammy."

Sammy just smiled, gracious and a little weary. When we got back to the house, he went up to his room at once. I heard his keyboard, the sweet, bluesy strains of the song he had been working on for Hannah, and was ashamed to have been so eager to offer him up to the genial Moloch of the national game.

George Johnson, meanwhile, hurried to the kitchen. Tomorrow his grandson and I would be flying home; but tonight the three of us were finally going to eat that meatloaf.

## fifteen

## home is the sailor

What I tell about "me," I tell about you.
The walls between us burned down long ago.
This voice seizing me is your voice
Burning to speak to us of us.

Rumi

———

*I had called ahead* and left a message on LeeAnne's machine, informing her of our arrival time, as instructed. I really had not known quite what to expect. But she was waiting at the gate at SFO when we got off the plane, as promised, quietly radiant and poised as ever, perhaps the least bit guarded in her Big Jack denim overalls and a 49ers sweatshirt, but still an anchor of familiar calm amid the airport ruckus. Sammy ran ahead to hug her and LeeAnne stooped to meet him, her glance meeting mine over his shoulder, a question in her eyes.

"Home is the sailor, home from the sea," I said.

"You got some sun."

"Nebraska is an oven, and New York is a humid oven. *You* look beautiful." She smiled, pleased and a bit less wary. As she straightened to embrace me, I surprised both of us and bent to kiss the denim expanse of her belly. "And how's our little girl?"

"Stay down there too long and she'll kick you in the mouth," LeeAnne said, stroking my head. She was delighted, but slightly embarrassed, conscious of being in public.

I straightened obligingly to kiss her in more standard airport-arrival fashion. Her lips were warm and firm and sweet with all the incomprehensible sweetness of the usual world. LeeAnne is right, perhaps, that a single life does not suffice to explain the richness of such moments. I felt as if I were waking from a dream—a coma, even, as Hannah had once: back from the heavens and the hells and the spirit's wandering, home to just this touch of beloved lips, and this sweet familiar flesh.

"Well!" LeeAnne murmured. "Well, well, well."

Sammy was already tugging at her arm. "The airplane movie was *really* slow," he told her. "Some kind of gushy love story."

LeeAnne and I exchanged a smile across the top of his head. We're always so relieved when the kid acts like an eight-year-old.

"You'll grow into that someday," LeeAnne said, taking his hand as I picked up our carry-on bag. "It takes a while to appreciate a love story."

Through the ride home, Sammy carried the conversational load, chattering away from the back seat. LeeAnne, turned to listen to him, glanced at me occasionally and raised an eyebrow or smiled, reading between the lines of the child version. The late-afternoon fog was tumbling over the hills west of 280, cool and gray and oddly soothing. Our old Toyota's rattles and creaks were soothing too, after the crisp, alien efficiency of the rental car.

Back at the house, LeeAnne had the vegetables of a simple stir-fry already chopped. Through dinner, we talked of her weekend's seminar, which had been a great success. After the meal, while I cleared the table and did the dishes, Sammy and LeeAnne spread a map of the United States out on the coffee table and he traced our route for her in minute, eventful detail for almost half an hour. They were just getting to New York when I finished the dishes. I left them alone and slipped away to my studio.

Everything was as I had left it, except for some signs of rummaging in the stacks of paintings leaning against the walls. LeeAnne had been through here with the buyer, of course, a man I had never met. But his eye had been painfully good— he had unerringly picked out three of my favorite works and taken them away. I already missed *Burning Music #17,* that desperate novice effort at synesthesia born of my first meeting with Hannah. I still had the phone number LeeAnne had given me in my pocket, but I knew I wasn't going to make the call. We cannot make our offerings to the world with strings attached. That much, at least, was clear.

My work-in-progress still stood on the easel at the center of the room. I took off the cover and considered it, unexpectedly pleased at the effect of the central flame. The canvas had ripened while I was gone, a good sign. It was warmer than I remembered, subtler, and more of a piece. The wild flare of yellow I had loosed the morning I left for Nebraska drew orange highlights out of the earthen depths of the rest of the canvas in a way I had not foreseen, and the structure's tension promised more surprise. I could feel the emptiness at the upper left, pregnant with a color I didn't know yet. Something cooling, maybe, a movement, a streaming blue.

In the studio's silence, I could hear the bathtub running down the hall. LeeAnne and Sammy had finished their debriefing and she was getting him ready for bed. I turned to the shelf that held my studio's cheap music system and found a tape of Hannah's—not the polished, bright, multi-tracked studio work of the album she'd released, but a coffeehouse basement tape made three years earlier, in the period just before the band came together, the songs sung solo, to one acoustic guitar, as I had known Hannah's music best. I put the tape in the machine and hit "Play," and there she was, the way she always said she would be, but in a way that only made me ache.

—

Hannah and I didn't see each other often in the years after Sammy was born. There was no avoidance—we were both absorbed in our lives, on our different coasts, and made our visits when we could. She was becoming a sort of phenomenon on the club scene by then and always had a gig somewhere. But when I did see her, it was like hearing the language of my homeland spoken.

Once, about three years after Sammy's birth, Hannah was on

the West Coast to play several clubs. She had arranged to play on one of her free days at the V.A. hospital in Napa County, something she had been doing occasionally since she began playing the guitar again after her accident. Hannah said the old veterans were the world's best audience.

We drove up to Yountville together on a Wednesday afternoon not long after the Fourth of July. LeeAnne stayed home with Sammy, who had the chicken pox, but she didn't begrudge me the trip into the Napa Valley summer heat in any case. LeeAnne and Hannah had reinvented their friendship yet again in the years since Sammy's birth; the three of us had returned, by the most unlikely route, to a condition close to those days in Utah when Hannah and Burton had come over on Friday nights for dinner and Scrabble. Hannah was good with Sammy in a hip, auntlike way, and she was easy with LeeAnne and ever more confident in herself. The three of us would put the kid to bed and drink a few beers in the kitchen and talk about God and art and destiny, as we always had, and laugh a lot. Hannah's eyes had the slightest crow's-foot crinkle at the corners now when she laughed. She'd cut her lush hair short, which actually made her look younger. She still wore jeans and baggy flannel lumberjack shirts, and when I hugged her good-bye I was still surprised by how slim she was beneath all her layers.

Then off she'd go, back to her life, and LeeAnne and I would do the dishes together and go back to ours. There is nothing like a child, I suppose, to put sexual tension in its place.

Away from the coast, the sun baked the summer-brown

hills. Hannah and I drove through fields of ripening grapes, listening to Lightnin' Hopkins. We stopped in Napa for lunch and were at the V.A. hospital in Yountville by two for Hannah's "gig": two dozen veterans of the Second World War and Korea and Vietnam, many of them in wheelchairs, parked in a little room with bad acoustics and a big TV set in the far corner. Several of the vets' gazes kept drifting to that set, from habit, even though it was turned off. Hannah played a bunch of Johnny Cash songs, some Hank Williams classics, and "The Ballad of the Green Berets," then did requests. The old veterans loved her. She faked her way through the Marine Corps Hymn and "Waltzing Matilda" and "The Battle of New Orleans" and finished with a rousing sing-along version of "The Caissons Go Rolling Along," with everybody, Hannah included, mumbling through the verses and shouting out the chorus.

When the show was over one of the Vietnam vets took Hannah and me out under the trees on the big rolling lawn and got us a little stoned. He had a blues harmonica and we goofed around with some vintage Dylan. When he went back inside to take some further medication for the voices in his head, Hannah and I wandered down the hill, across the green grass, until we came to the dusty cemetery.

The late-afternoon sun was still hot. We walked slowly among the rows of weathered white marble markers, reading the inscriptions dating back to the Spanish–American War. Every grave had a small American flag stuck in the ground beside it, left over from the Fourth of July.

At last we sought shelter from the sun in the thin shade of

a foothill oak. Farther down the hill, the golden-brown cemetery lawn ran into woods. Above the valley a red-tailed hawk made a great lazy arc on motionless wings.

"Do you remember the cemetery in Utah, that day you stormed out of the cafeteria after your fight with Burton?" I said. "How we sat there so long under the trees, without saying a word, with the snow coming down?"

Hannah glanced at me and smiled. "Of course."

"That was the day I knew I was in big trouble with you. That was the day I knew I loved you."

"It's funny," Hannah said. "That was the day I knew you would be my friend."

I felt a gentle flare of sadness at that; it seemed a trifle dry, on the whole; but I knew how hard we'd worked to be the friends we were, and that she was right to underline it. We were silent. The light was growing rich, as the hard glare of afternoon softened toward evening. All around us, the tiny flags hung motionless in the still summer air, rank upon rank, beside the graying stones. Two hills over, a vineyard's staked vines made their own quiet rows, marshalled, orderly, heavy with the season's fruit.

At last I stirred. "We should get back. LeeAnne was going to hold dinner for us."

Hannah stood up and brushed the dust off her butt. Our eyes met, as they had a thousand times, and she smiled.

"I lied," she said. "I knew I loved you that first night, at Burton's grandfather's house. Remember? Right by the fireplace. You came up to me after I sang 'White Empty Canvas,' and asked me who had written that song, as if it mattered to you."

"Oh, I remember," I said. "Of course I remember. I loved you when you said that it was you."

—

By the time Sammy was five, Hannah's band was finally coming together. I saw her even less, then, as all her time went into practice and all her money went into equipment, and yet in some way we were closer than ever. In *Moby-Dick*, Ishmael talks about an old whaling technique for cutting the blubber off a whale at sea, in which one man would be out working on the dead whale with a big knife, while the other, still on the ship, was connected to him with a line called a monkey-rope. And so I felt about Hannah. I would watch her on the stage, with Sammy on my lap and LeeAnne at my side, and it seemed to me while she sang that some unbreakable monkey-rope still linked my life with hers, for better and for worse, and that I felt every rise and fall of the sea between us, affecting us both. She did her work and I did mine and somehow the work was the same and there was no room in it for missing her. When we saw each other, after however many weeks or months, it was less like meeting after being apart and more like continuing something that had simply gone on in a different way while we concentrated on other things, as if the rope that joined us had gone slack for a while, and then grown taut again.

The last time I saw her was at the house she shared with Pete Michaels, the other lead guitarist in her band, in a little coastal Connecticut town. I'd been in New York for a few days to open a show in SoHo and was leaving for the West Coast the next morning. The band was also leaving the next day, to begin their grassroots tour. The CD had just come out, the first single was already getting good airplay, and everyone was jolly. The van stood half-loaded in the driveway and people kept putting things into it through most of the night; they were due to leave at dawn. But there was quite a bit of beer fueling the process, and no small amount of weed, and by midnight or so all work had ceased. Pete—a gentle, lovely man who was astonishingly deft with a guitar—and the others retreated to the garage and began jamming away, a slow build that gradually grew rowdy and hilarious.

Hannah and I walked down the path to sit by the little river that wound sluggishly through the third-growth woods about fifty yards from the house. As the music behind us soared and dipped and wavered like a drunken gull, we sat sipping our beers and slapping the occasional mosquito. The full moon lay on the water in a long, unbroken silver sheen. My show had opened to mild success; for the first time in twenty years I had paintings hanging in New York with SOLD stickers on them. And the Blue Flame Band was about to hit the road. It was a moment of sweetness.

"This is what I was so afraid of," I marveled.

Hannah glanced at me. "Hmm?"

"Remember that afternoon on Mount Tam?—the peak, in the bright sunlight. You knew it was time to come down and do the work, and I fought it. I was so afraid of losing everything I loved in that moment. But *this* is what I was afraid of—

you see? This moment in the valley, in the dark, with nothing but work to do on the road ahead. And look at that moonlight."

"I never saw a moment like this ahead of us," Hannah said. It was almost a concession. "All I saw was heat and flame."

A whippoorwill made its haunting call nearby. Through the trees, Pete took the jam somewhere new, breathtakingly—out on a limb, in the wilderness of the G blues scale, he built and built, going nowhere, seemingly, running out of anywhere to go.

"What's he going to do with *that?*" I laughed.

"God knows," Hannah said, pleased with her lover. "Petey sure doesn't."

A full round past the point of no return, Pete brought it home by a simple route that seemed obvious only after the fact. We heard the others laughing and exclaiming, as they settled back into a bass rhythm.

"They need another guitar," Hannah said.

"I think I'll just stay here, if you don't mind. This moonlight…"

Hannah smiled her understanding and kissed my cheek. She took the flashlight with her and made her way back up the path. I heard her Telecaster kick in a moment later, a surefooted riff along the edge of some whole new precipice. The band went with her easily, beautifully, following Hannah's lead, focused suddenly and sobering in the music. And on the river's surface, the moon's twice-reflected light made a different beauty, shimmering silver on the invisible movement of the stream.

—

The tape player in my studio clicked off. In the silence, I could hear Sammy's keyboard in his bedroom down the hall. He was trying out his Hannah song on LeeAnne.

He was still working on it, I noted—the refrain was a little uncertain and the bridge was weak. But then, he'd probably be working on it for quite some time to come.

I picked up my palette and started playing with some blues, starting with a mid-morning sky and adding purple, deepening the shade, inevitably, toward indigo. But that wasn't going to do it, I could see almost at once—the canvas wanted something new.

LeeAnne came to the doorway. "Busy?"

"Going nowhere fast. Come on in."

She crossed the floor, shuffling in her red slippers. I leaned back against the table and she slipped into the circle of my arm; I rested my other hand lightly on the round shelf of her belly. The baby stirred, thrillingly, beneath my hand, and something in me answered, moved as if to prayer, *Sweet little girl, on your way into this world of beauty and of death, I will give you all the love I can.*

We stood for a while looking at the canvas. LeeAnne smelled of green peppers and something sweet.

"It's like it's been ten thousand years since I've seen you," she said. "I hardly know where to begin."

I was still looking at the canvas, at that flare of hungry flame at the heart of it, that was going to burn up everything I thought I knew about blue. But the painting wasn't going anywhere. The real things stay, and stay, and when they go, they stay as grief.

"I know what you mean," I said, and turned my face into her hair. It seemed to me there was time enough for everything.

Be careful what you pray for, I suppose. I had vowed in Utah, in those days when indigo sufficed, that if I had to stand in fire to see like that for the rest of my life, I would. And so, in my way, I have—every day now at the canvas, confronted by my own ongoing failure in the face of beauty's ever-new demands, I stand and burn. And even now, every time I think of Hannah, that living flame renews itself, if I don't flinch before how terrible it can be. I can even hear her voice sometimes through the crackle of it, rich and sweet and strangely innocent, soothing something in me like honeyed tea. She is still sitting with her guitar on the stool with the uneven legs, in front of the big cold window that faced the mountains, warming the room with a quiet song. Her face is soft and clear and perfectly intent, her hands are sure, and the light is good. It is late afternoon, but there is no tomorrow in that music, and there is no yesterday, and there is nothing else in all the world I want.